The

Par

Sara Alexi is the author of ....eek Village Series and the
Greek Island Series

.

She divides her time between England and a small village
in Greece.

http://facebook.com/authorsaraalexi

Sara Alexi

THE VILLAGE IDIOTS

Part 1 - Inheritance

oneiro

Published by Oneiro Press 2017

ISBN: 9781522012085

Also by Sara Alexi

Chapter 1

'Well, here's to the old man. Safe journeys, George,' Spiros mutters as he turns his glass, the condensation wetting his dirt-ingrained fingers. He asked for a strawberry milkshake but now he wishes it was chocolate. With a cupped hand he wipes the pink froth off his moustache and concentrates, trying to control his right eyelid, which has started twitching. He turns his face away so that Takis cannot see.

'Yes, here's to Captain George!' Takis raises his ouzo glass, the ice chiming against the sides, turning the aniseed liquid a milky white as it melts.

They tap the rims against each other.

'To George,' they say in unison, and they look out at the sea.

The scene before them is a blend of blues: the glinting silver-blue of the sea, the hazy blue-purple of the hills on the far side of the bay, and the deep, heat-heavy blue of the sky. Seeming to float in the middle of the bay of the broad inlet, a white frill keeping it from sinking, is the small island fort. Spiros watches a boat laden with tourists puttering its way out to the fort, its wake fanning out, rippling the calm water until, a little to his annoyance, a group of women line up on the quayside, blocking his view.

One of this group poses for her friend to take a picture of her with the island fort in the background.

Another has plucked a menu from the next table and she huddles over it with another woman who could be her twin, right in his line of vision. The air is now scented with a mixture of chemicals, unnatural. Spiros notices, as he holds his breath, that Takis breathes in deeply, as if he likes the smell, and smiles at the group of women, running his hand over his balding head, plastering the long wisps of hair over his crown.

'So …' Spiros says to distract Takis before he starts talking to the women.

Takis likes to talk to people they don't know, women especially, and Spiros never quite understands the jokes he makes with them. When it is not jokes, Takis talks in riddles that don't quite make sense to him but which often make the women giggle nervously. And always, always, it results in one of the women becoming upset and Takis being in a bad mood for the rest of the day.

'So, they just found him in the boat then?' Spiros taps Takis's knee to get his attention.

'On the floor at the bottom of the steps, down in the saloon, I understand. Heart attack – pretty instant, they reckon.'

Takis sits up, straightens his back as the women arrange themselves in the seats at the table next to them. Spiros puts his arms around the backs of the chairs either side of him, creating a wall between the women and Takis. There is a faint smell of body odour – he must change his shirt tomorrow, or the next day. The women move in unison to sit at another table.

'I hope for George's sake it was instant.' Spiros does not like the thought of George suffering. Not that he was a close friend, but he didn't talk slowly to Spiros or

4

ignore him like a lot of people do. He treated him as if he was just another friend and so Spiros liked him for that. When Takis brought him to Saros, they would usually find George sitting here at the café, waiting for business, just across from where his yacht was parked, ready to take tourists out for a trip in the bay, or, occasionally, overnight to Orino Island.

'Where is his boat – have they moved it?' Spiros looks up the harbour edge to his right.

'Yacht. And yes, the port police moved it,' Takis says, and he points along the harbour wall to the left, where a shiny new yacht is just coming in to tie up.

George's boat looks old by comparison, the white hull slightly yellowing, the deck covered in frayed ropes. The fenders hanging from the sides are scuffed and partially deflated, the blue paint, top and bottom, all but worn away. In all, it is a bit of a mess, now he really takes the time to look at it. But then, Captain George himself was not a tidy man: scruffy white hair, grubby jeans cut off at the bottom, as he was too short to get any to fit properly. His fisherman's cap that never left his head was shiny with age and he always smelt of stale cigarette smoke. But George always had a tale to tell, and his tales were easy to understand, and often they would make him laugh. That, and he would often buy Spiros a pack of mints, for no reason, just because he was kind. Mind you, he wasn't the only one. Vasso gives him mints too, and often she mutters that it is not right for a grown man to have to ask for money from his friend. She means Takis. But Takis is just taking care of him, isn't he?

'I guess we'll miss George,' Spiros says.

'Indeed I will.' Takis nods his head.

'He never did take us for a ride on his boat, did he?'

'Yacht,' Takis corrects.

'Can you imagine owning a yacht?' Spiros ponders.

'Life would be a breeze, eh?' Takis chuckles at the thought. 'No more counting every penny, working odd jobs. We'd be made up, eh? Go and do a bit of fishing, take the occasional tourist out. He had it made, did that George, poor man.'

They sit in silence again. The tourist boat returns from the island fort and the captain ties up to the pier, sits on the bollard he has tied to and plays with his worry beads. His boat fills slowly with a new cargo of passengers and after half an hour he pushes off again. People wander past along the waterfront: couples, families, an old man with a dog. Spiros sucks at his straw, teasing out the last of the milkshake from the bottom of the glass.

A cat slinks between the tables, winds its body around Takis's chair. Spiros holds his hand out to encourage it; Takis hisses at the animal, stamps his foot to frighten it away. Spiros frowns.

'Gentlemen,' the waiter addresses them. 'My shift is about to end – can you settle the bill, please?'

'Oh yeah, right.' Takis fumbles in his pocket, takes out a few coins, counts them carefully and hands them over.

'That's it, I'm broke,' he says when the waiter has gone.

'Broke?' Spiros asks.

'Yup, no more milkshakes for you.'

'But what about all those gold sovereigns?' He can feel his eyelid start to twitch.

'Gone, sold the last one last month.'

'Last month? But they're gold, right? They're worth hundreds and hundreds?'

'I wish! No, but I've had a good run with them, I managed to make each one last a month.' He sounds proud. 'But all good things come to an end, and that little inheritance has all gone now.' He sighs loudly and shakes his head. 'Back looking for odd jobs, I guess.'

'But it's only July! There'll be no orange or olive picking for months.' The twitching is getting worse.

'Stop it.' Takis points at him. Spiros puts his hand to his eye to hold the offending muscle steady.

'We've always been all right, so don't you worry. Mates stand by each other. You have to think of us as a team. I'm the brains and you're the brawn.'

Spiros likes it when Takis talks like that – it makes him feel safe. He doesn't see Takis as a father figure, even though Takis is his senior by more than ten years and what little hair he has left is white. No, he is more of an older brother who looks out for him.

Spiros's hand drops from his face and his breathing steadies.

'Right, that's better. So, tomorrow we'll put the word out that we're looking for work again.'

They watch the tourist boat bob its way across to the island fort, the antlike people disembarking and filtering into a single line that circumnavigates the stonework.

'Yes, we had a good run.' Takis laughs. 'Considering we very nearly didn't have those coins at all.'

He laughs again, and when Spiros doesn't join in the merriment he adds, 'I told you about the hot water tank, right?'

'What hot water tank?'

'Spiro, I've told you a hundred times! Your memory is like a sieve.' Takis knocks back the last of his ouzo and smacks his lips in satisfaction.

'Tell me again.' Spiros can remember parts of the story – in fact, he can remember a lot of the tale but he can never remember the detail, and it is the detail that takes him away to another place inside his head where he can watch it happening and it all feels so real. George's tales did that too. He is going to miss George.

'Okay, so the gold was bought by my papous, after the war. They were hard times. The drachma wasn't worth much, and he didn't trust the banks … But gold, that was real, solid. Papous was a smart man, and he had a factory in Athens that made motorbikes. You know, those three-wheeled bikes? You don't see them much any more, but there were lots of them then. Oh, I know who's got one – you know Thanasis who keeps the donkeys? He's got one, in his orchard, under the trees. It doesn't work any more, but you'll have seen it when we've been round there.'

Spiros nods, but he can't really remember having seen the bike. When they visit Thanasis, he's always far more interested in the donkeys.

'Anyway, he had this factory,' Takis continues, 'and he did all right, and apparently each time he sold one he would use some of the money to buy a sovereign, and he tucked them all away. Over the years the number of sovereigns grew and grew and then he died, leaving my yiayia with instructions to keep them safe for a rainy day.'

There's a faded black-and-white picture of Takis's papous and yiayia on the wall in his house. Takis's papous looks stern, serious, but his yiayia has a soft face that looks a bit like a feminine version of Takis.

'Well, such a responsibility worried her. She'd never had to deal with money up to that point, it was all left to the men. So she turned to my baba, who was in his twenties then, and she asked him to hide them. "Put them somewhere not even I could find them," she told him, and so he did, and she never asked where because she felt it was safer that way.'

Takis stops to chuckle and picks up his glass of ouzo only to find it empty, and he puts it down again with a frown.

'Well, one day my baba was out at work, and Yiayia was in the kitchen cooking or whatever, and the water wouldn't run hot. So she went round to one of the neighbours, who was a plumber, and asked him to come and have a look.'

Spiros likes this next bit of the story but he does his best to sit still.

'The neighbour came and had a look at the water heater, and he declared that it was broken and not worth repairing and that he would put in a new one.'

Spiros squirms in his seat.

9

'So the old tank was taken out and a new one put in, and the water heated up fine, and the plumber took away the old tank and the bits of pipe, and Yiayia did the dishes and the washing and made a meal, and when my baba came home she told him all about the excitement of her day, and the new water tank, and what a mess she'd had to clean up after the plumber …

'Well, when he heard this he stood up so fast his chair fell over! "My God, woman, what have you done!" my baba cried out, and then he told her that he had hidden the sovereigns in the water tank. It was the safest place he could think of, and certainly not somewhere anyone would think to look! Of course, she immediately burst into floods of tears and begged his forgiveness. "Never mind that now," he said. "Which plumber, and where is his yard?" So she told him which plumber it was, but my baba was not a stupid man, and he knew that if he explained the whole situation to the plumber there was a chance that the water tank would disappear and he would never see the gold coins again. No, he had to be cunning, and so, in the dead of night, he broke into the yard with a torch, where he found hundreds of old boilers stacked up in a corner!'

Spiros can picture him, his face shining in the moonlight, his moustache just a jagged black line to his sideburns, looking this way and that, creeping on tiptoe like a cartoon burglar.

Takis continues. 'So there he was, lit up in the moonlight, using his torch to see more clearly, shaking each water tank in turn, listening for the coins rattling around inside. He could only hope it was the sovereigns and not a bit of old pipe, or some other loose bit of metal. After all, the boilers all looked pretty much the same and he couldn't tell for sure which was his. Well, he found one that rattled, but he couldn't get the tank open there and then, so he had to throw it over the yard wall, follow it over and then run home with it cradled in his arms.'

'How did he get it open?' Spiros loves this part; he remembers it clearly now.

'Well, I was never sure he was telling the truth about this, but he always told me that he dropped it off the balcony. They lived in Athens in a flat that was three floors up, and he always said he got Yiayia to go down onto the street and then he pushed the tank off the balcony. It hit the road so hard that it burst open, but the force also broke open the case he had put the coins in, and then the tank started to roll off down the hill and the coins spilled out all over the place like a rabbit does its droppings.'

Spiros is delighted. 'Like a rabbit does its droppings,' he repeats, and he starts to laugh.

'Yiayia ran off down the hill after the tank, plucking up the coins one by one and putting them in her apron pocket.'

'Like golden rabbit droppings,' Spiros says again.

'So you see, they might have been gone forever, but as luck would have it they were not, and they came to me when baba died, and I have to say we've done alright the past two years on them, you and me.'

He grins and then his cheeks grow slack and his mouth loses form. 'But now, my friend, we need to save what little we have left, so no bus for us. It's the path along the shore instead. Let's go back to the village.'

'So no chicken dinner at Stella's tonight then?' Spiros asks as they begin the walk.

'Not even coffee at Theo's *kafenio*, my friend.' Takis tries to throw an arm around his shoulder but Spiros is taller than he is and bigger across the shoulders, and so it is Spiros who puts an arm across Takis's shoulders and pulls him in for a hug.

'Get off, you big brute, you don't know your own strength!' Takis breaks free, laughing, his cheeks a reddish hue.

'We can go to my mama's for dinner,' Spiros suggests.

'I still don't think I'm in your mama's good books, Spiro, not since we did that job that landed us in the police station.'

'But you explained that to her, and it wasn't as if we were arrested.'

'Your mama watches out for you, Spiro, which is a good thing, but she has a long memory and I don't think she is ever going to approve of me. She certainly seems to dwell on the things I've done.'

'So what are we going to eat, then?'

'Maybe you should go to your mama's. I think I have some lentils, I'll be fine.'

The town is behind them now, the sea lapping by their feet on their left, and to the right the orange orchards are thick, the oranges at this time of year no bigger than chestnuts, hard and green. Spiros likes this bit of the walk. There is a spot where the currents bring in all sorts of flotsam and jetsam. He found a headless doll once, and a baby's bottle, which he offered to a lady with a baby in the village. For some reason, she didn't want it. He watches his feet as he walks to see what treasure he might find today.

'Maybe we can do a little fishing tomorrow, if we don't find work,' Takis suggests, 'off the end of the jetty in the village. Then, if we catch anything and we cannot sell it, we can always eat it.'

He is walking with his hands in his pockets, legs swinging freely, as if he has all the time in the world, which perhaps they do. Spiros puts his hands in his pockets, too, copies Takis's walk, and forgets to look for treasure, and then finds he is past that point and can now see the jetty on the outskirts of the village. Sometimes he doesn't mind fishing, but usually he finds it boring. It's hard to sit still for as long as is needed.

'I hope we find work,' he says.

'I'm sure we'll find work. I'll go and see Grigoris first thing tomorrow morning. He often has jobs he needs doing on his land. And if not, we can try Aleko. We can run errands for him, or hold his spanners as he works or something.'

'Or roll tyres into the corner. I enjoyed that.'

'Something will turn up,' Takis reassures him, and Spiros believes him, but his eyelid starts to twitch anyway.

There are two small fishing boats tied to the jetty, and under it, where it joins the land, a heap of fishing nets have been stuffed. If they come tomorrow, though, they won't use a boat, or a net; instead, they will sit on the end of the pier with a line and a hook, for hours and hours.

The path turns inland between the orange trees, skirting along the edge of the village and onto a lane that leads to the main square. Their houses are on the other side of the square, behind Babis the lawyer's house.

Their two whitewashed stone cottages stand next to each other, identical in layout, with two rooms at the front and another room with a separate entrance at the back. They are perhaps the oldest cottages in the village. They had electricity installed a few years ago, but there is still no heating for the winter and only a layer of tiles between them and the sun in the summer. Takis was born and grew up in his house, and his back room is full to the rafters with things he might need, or perhaps sell, one day. Spiros and his mama moved into their house when his baba died. In her grief, his mama shut herself away in the single back room, and Spiros was left the two rooms at the front. It is just as well that there is no rent to pay. His uncle, whose house it is, said something about how looking after his mama and keeping house would 'make a man of him', which he didn't understand.

'I'm going to America for a year,' the uncle said, 'and you can use the house till I get back' – but that was eight years ago.

At first, the arrangement worried Spiros, who didn't want to disappoint his uncle by not becoming a man, and he worried about where they would live when the uncle did come back. But now he wonders if his uncle will ever come back; besides, no one can doubt he is a man now, with a proper moustache and even some white in his hair, in the bit that will not lay flat on his head.

Is it true to say, he wonders, that it is fortunate that he lives next to Takis? Or is it the other way around, and they are friends because they live next door? Either way, Takis has been a good friend. It was hard at first in the days after his baba's death, when his mama would not even get out of bed and could see no point to life. He had struggled with the basics, like cooking, and washing their clothes. But Takis had shown him there was no need to cook when Stella's eatery made such good chicken and chips, and no need to wash the clothes when he could take them to a woman in the village who would do it for him for a few coins. And for a few more coins, Kyria Isodia comes to his part of the house once a week to tidy and clean. Takis seemed to know how to organise things, and his way did take away much of the worry. But it also meant that the small allowance his uncle sent was usually spent before it arrived.

Yup, tomorrow they will definitely have to find some work.

Chapter 2

As they walk through the square, the smell of chicken and chips greets them and Spiros feels himself drawn to fill the empty cavity that is his stomach. How nice it would be to flop down in one of the eatery's wooden chairs, cool himself with a beer and tuck into Stella's food. The fairy lights Stella has wound around the twisted tree outside the eatery call to him. Their tiny twinkles always give him a little thrill, a promise of good things. Well, it is always good at Stella's, so it isn't just a promise – it's the truth!

Two of the four tables on the pavement either side of the tree are occupied, each with a group of four people. Both doors to the building stand open: the double ones to the grill, where you can watch your takeaway being wrapped, and the single door that opens into the second, smaller room, with four tables. From this door comes a roar of laughter – farmers, no doubt – and Spiros wishes even more that they could go there, be part of the crowd, become lost in the humour and storytelling.

'Look away, Spiro,' Takis says as they cross the square. 'It is not for us today.' He waves at Vasso in her kiosk in the centre of the square and pats his chest pocket, where he keeps his cigarettes. This action usually precedes a detour to Vasso's little wooden shop, where Takis will talk in meaningless riddles and make jokes he cannot understand. But Takis carries on past the kiosk today and starts up the lane that leads to their houses. They must be really broke.

'Well, there's luck!' Takis exclaims.

Babis, the 'Lawyer for the People', as he likes to call himself, is just locking the side door to his house as they approach.

'Hello, boys.' He is all white teeth and he shakes hands first with Takis and then with Spiros. He smells even more strongly of chemicals than the women in Saros did.

'How are you doing, Babi?' Takis asks.

'Fine. Fine. Terrible about George, though! Such a shock, such a shock.'

'Ah well, if he had to go, that was the way he would have wanted it, on his boat, still working. He would have hated to get so old he could do nothing but sit, so perhaps it is for the best. But I will miss him.'

'Indeed, indeed.'

Babis does not sound like he really has any feelings for George.

'And where are you boys going?' Babis continues.

Spiros snorts. He is a man, not a boy.

'Just on our way home. I would be happy to invite you but the cupboards are a little bare at the moment.' Takis makes it sound so inconsequential. Spiro's stomach rumbles.

'Have you eaten?' Babis says with a hand on Takis's shoulder. Takis shakes his head. 'Well, come and be

17

my guests at Stella's. I have a little something I wanted to talk to you about anyway.'

'I don't mind if we do,' Takis says, and he gives Spiros a conspiratorial wink, leans towards him and whispers through the side of his mouth, 'I told you we'd be okay.'

But Spiros frowns and looks sideways at Babis. He has not asked them to eat with him for no reason. Why is he making such an offer? There is something about the man he does not like; he seems sneaky, sly.

There is some discussion as they reach Stella's as to whether they should sit inside or out. Spiros wants to go in, to the talking and laughter, but Babis presses them to sit outside, insisting once again that they need to talk. It will be quieter, he says. For Spiros it is a small let-down but at least he will get a chicken dinner.

'Hello.' Stella is quick to come and greet them. She has an apron over her floral dress and she is wiping her hands on a blue-and-white tea towel. The colours match those of the tables and chairs.

'Chicken and chips all round, boys?'

Spiros does not mind Stella calling him a boy. From her it sounds like a term of endearment, not a judgement. Once she returns inside, her voice echoes from the high ceiling as she repeats their order to her husband Mitsos, who, no doubt, will be behind the grill. Spiros likes Mitsos. Mitsos takes the time to talk to him, usually about his goats, and quite often after such a chat, he offers him the job of herding them the following day. Maybe Spiros should go in and ask if he could mind the goats tomorrow.

He is about to ask Takis what he thinks of the idea when his friend says very grandly, 'So, Babi, what was it you wanted to talk about?'

But then, as if he is not in the least interested in the answer, he stretches in the way he always does before he eats. His fills his lungs and his chest expands. He rubs either side of his ribcage with both hands and then, not lifting his palms away, he pats his stomach with his fingers as he exhales.

'Ah yes,' Babis says, and then he pauses as Stella returns with three beers, the tops of which she pops off, scooping the caps into the pocket of her apron.

'Well,' Babis continues after she is gone, 'as we said, poor George. But it is an ill wind that blows no one any good, and my humble law firm has the honour of handling his estate.'

'What's an estate?' Spiros interjects.

'Property, what he owned,' Takis explains impatiently. Then, turning back to Babis, he adds, 'It will go to his sister in America, right?'

'I thought so.' Babis looks up into the leaves of the tree. 'An easy job, I thought, so I called her.' He shakes and then nods his head at the memory. 'You know what she told me? She told me she wanted nothing. She officially revoked her right to the inheritance.'

'*What?* Why would she do that? That boat is worth money, right?' Takis says.

'Says she doesn't want to own property in Greece. Says she won't get involved in the Greek tax system again for a scrappy old boat. Her words, not mine … Oh, thank you, Stella.'

19

Spiros loves the way Stella can carry three, sometimes four plates of food, one in each hand, one on each forearm. She is a tiny person, arms and legs as thin as a bird's, and yet she seems so strong for her size when she does this. She puts his plate before him and he notices that she has given him extra lemon sauce.

'Thank you, Stella,' he calls after her as she disappears back inside.

Her head reappears: 'You're welcome Spiro!' She smiles and is gone.

'So what do you do with his stuff, then – does the government take it?' Takis asks as he unwraps his knife and fork from the paper serviette that binds them together.

'Ha ha! I wish it had been that simple. No, it was my job to chase down the nearest relatives.' Babis shoves a forkful of chicken into his mouth, leaving lemon sauce running down his chin.

'I was not aware he had any relatives round here. He always used to moan about his lack of family.' Takis has discarded his cutlery, picking his chicken leg up with his fingers instead. He gnaws round the bone, pulling on tendons, his rosy lips shining with the grease.

'It turns out he did – or rather, does – have some very distant relatives right here in the village. You know, through marriage and so on.' Babis sounds excited, as if he is telling a joke and is about to get to the punchline.

'Oh yeah?' Takis swills his food down with beer, drinking straight from the bottle.

'Can you guess who?' Babis pauses, his fork mid-air, waiting for an answer.

20

'Not a clue. Who?' Takis says, the bottle of beer to his lips again.

'Well, actually there are two, of equal relationship to George, very distant, several cousins removed. You must be able to guess who I mean now?'

Babis's eyes twinkle and he puts another forkful of food into his mouth and chews. Spiros watches the food going round in his mouth.

'Nope!' Takis drinks his beer.

'Why, you and Spiros here!' Babis says, grinning broadly.

Takis's eyes grow wide at this, and his beer sprays across the table and into Spiros's face and all over his plate.

'You serious?' He sounds amazed, and he even forgets to apologise for the puddle of beer that Spiros's chicken now sits in.

Spiros dabs at his face with a paper napkin from the holder. The beer shower has consumed his attention but he is sure something important was just said.

'Absolutely serious,' Babis replies. 'More beer?' He puts his hand up to attract Stella's attention.

'You mean his – his ...' Takis seems to be struggling to get the next word out.

'Yes, his boat, but I'm afraid there was not much else really. Masses of paperwork, just records about the boat dating back ten years and more. I've not been through the lot yet, but yes, you and Spiros here are now joint owners of George's yacht. Well, you will be when probate has gone through. I'll be as quick as I can with the legal stuff.'

Babis thanks Stella for his beer and raises his bottle.

'To George,' he says, and Takis automatically clinks bottles with him, still too stunned to speak.

'Are you sure?' Takis asks finally.

'As sure as I can be, and I'll tell you another thing for nothing, I'm not doing the paperwork again. If someone else wants to prove there is a closer relative, they can help themselves, but as for me I'm done. You are the relatives and that is that!'

'George's boat!' Takis doesn't sound like he normally sounds; his voice is all high-pitched.

'When probate goes through,' Babis adds, to qualify the point.

'You hear that, Spiro? We own George's boat!'

'What's all the excitement about?' Stella calls across from where she is clearing one of the other tables.

'It's your news to tell, not mine,' Babis says to Takis.

'Stella!' Takis is on his feet. 'Spiros and I own George's yacht!'

He takes her hands, and before Spiros can understand what is happening, Takis is jigging around in a circle, taking Stella with him. Round and round they go, and it looks fun, so Spiros stands too and Takis takes his hand and for a second the three of them spin until finally Stella breaks free.

'Well, boys, there's a surprise! Can you sail?' she asks, laughing.

Spiros stops dancing. He has never even been on a boat.

'Not yet.' Takis does not seem to see this as a problem.

'Well, let me be the first to congratulate you! Have you finished here?' She looks over at the empty plates on their table.

'Thanks, Stella,' Babis says. 'So boys, if you can come to my office, or pass by my house, I have some papers you will need to sign, and I'll need some ID.'

'But you know who we are,' Spiros says.

'It's how it's done,' Takis answers, and there's something in the way he says it that Spiros does not like. Takis said the words slowly, as if he was speaking to someone who is deaf or something.

Spiros feels something on his shoulder and he turns to find Stella is patting his back. Then she rubs his shoulder as if he has hurt himself, which feels nice even though he hasn't, and it softens Takis's words.

In Saros again, they wander down to the waterfront, watching the sun start its descent into the sea, the colours all soft and pinkish in the sky and in the water. Babis gave them a lift in, and they sat in his office whilst he sorted through piles of papers on his enormous desk. Then he made them sign – 'here, and here, and here' – and now they have come to the harbour to look at George's boat. Their boat.

'There she is, our yacht!' Takis stops on the quayside, hands thrust into his pockets, across from the old boat. Spiros looks at the ropes that attach the boat to the pier – a black one that is very worn, and a white one that is now grey with age.

'Is it really ours?' Spiros asks.

'She sure is! You want to go aboard?'

'Can we? Is it allowed?'

'As I said, she is ours, and we can do as we like.'

How often he has wanted to go aboard. George told him that there are steps that go down below and inside there is a tiny kitchen and even a toilet. He said there were cabins with beds and that you can sleep inside, and yet from the outside it doesn't look big enough to fit all these things inside. He cannot wait to see.

'Babis said something about needing to do some papers first.' It doesn't feel right somehow that they are allowed on.

'Legal stuff, bureaucracy. The boat is ours, I tell you.'

Looking at the boat more carefully now than he has in the past, Spiros notices that it isn't as white or as shiny as he had always thought. In fact, it all looks a little old and grubby. The back of the boat is facing the pier, and its front points out to sea, ready to set off! The two ropes, the white one and the black one, come from the back corners of the yacht, dipping down in an arc almost to the water, and then back up again to where they are tied to iron rings set into the concrete.

24

Takis bends down and picks up the fraying black rope; pulling it hand over hand, he brings the boat closer to the pier.

'Pull the white rope.'

He keeps hold of his rope with one hand and points with the other to the rope holding the boat at the other side. Spiros takes the rope that was once white and is now grey and pulls. He can remember watching on occasion as George brought the boat into the harbour. He would bring it in backward. The anchor would be dropped with a splash into the water a long way out, and one of the tourists would stand at the front of the boat pressing buttons on the controller as George steered them in. The chain would come clanking out of the front of the boat, lowering the anchor down into the water. George would shout at the tourist and the tourist would shout back. Bringing the boat in always involved a lot of shouting. Setting off in the morning was the opposite; that was a smooth and silent affair.

As he and Takis pull on the ropes, the boat comes toward the pier a little way, but then the anchor chain at the bow stretches out tight, and the yacht refuses to come any closer. Takis lets go of his rope now, and the boat starts to drift away from the pier again, but there is just enough time for him to hop across the gap, and he is on board! Spiros watches as he unties a rope and carefully lowers what looks like a scaffolding plank across the gap. The end of the wooden board lands with a thunk on the concrete, forming a narrow bridge across to the yacht.

'On you come,' Takis says and he puts his foot on the edge of the plank to stabilise it. There is a makeshift handrail of cord laced across metal uprights. Spiros takes hold of this for stability, but it wobbles so he lets go and trusts his balance instead. With three long steps he is on board.

At the back of the yacht is the seat where George used to sit, behind the big shiny wheel that steers the vessel. They are standing on this seat now, and Takis rests a hand on the wheel, but when it moves he quickly takes it off. The sliding hatch that gives access to the rooms down below is firmly shut, and the sails are all folded away. The deck, even to Spiros's eyes, is a mess, with frayed ropes heaped here and there, and the deck itself is yellow in some parts and grey in others. But despite this, in the pit of his stomach a quiver of excitement rises and escapes from his throat as a squeal of excitement.

'Yup, First Mate Spiro, welcome aboard!'

'Aye aye, Captain,' he answers, and another squeal escapes him.

'I told you something would turn up, didn't I?' Takis says, and he steps around the wheel, down into the cockpit, where he sits, putting his feet up on the seat opposite.

Spiros goes the other way around the wheel, sits opposite Takis and puts his feet up too. He copies the way Takis spreads his arms along the back of the seat, taking up as much space as possible.

'We are yacht owners now, Spiro, my friend! Men of wealth, the idle rich. We are sitting on a gold mine and it is ours, all ours.' Takis puts back his head and laughs.

'It is fun and everything, but are we really the owners, Taki? I mean, really, *really*? Can we take tourists out like George and sit at the café when we have no work, and no longer take jobs like that drain cleaning we once did and that yard clearing when we didn't get paid, and

26

do we no longer have to spend the winter picking other people's oranges and olives?'

'Spiro, we really, really do own this beast, and yes, we can sit back and take life easy. Once probate has gone through, the possibilities are endless.'

Spiros is too excited to remain sitting; he wants to explore the metal rail around the bow, look at the ropes coiled up by the mast, walk the length of the yacht, look down at the anchor chain that is visible in the clear water, all the way to the bottom.

'Can you imagine if we got a group of Swedish girls?' Takis calls to him. There are three ropes that come out of holes in the mast and through pulleys at the bottom, and they are tied very tight, as if they are securing something very heavy. Spiros looks but does not touch.

'How are we going to learn what all these ropes do?' he calls back to Takis.

Chapter 3

'No, you cannot sail her.' The port police man is emphatic.

Spiros looks around the room. They are on the upper floor of one of the big, grand houses on the seafront. The walls are panelled in delicately carved wood, and the room looks like it was once a fine dining room. Desks are packed in wherever they can fit. The desktops overflow with paperwork and there are bulletin boards on the wall with all sorts of notices pinned to them. All along one wall, large windows stretch from floor to ceiling, giving an almost uninterrupted view of the water, up to where the bay continues beyond the village in one direction and all the way out to sea the other way. The island fort sits centrally in this vista.

'But she will be ours when the paperwork is done,' Takis argues. 'It is just a formality.'

It was Lazarus who suggested they come to speak to the port police, and he steps forward now. He wears a suit and talks in a low voice.

'Look,' he says, 'we are three friends of George's and we just thought it would be a nice tribute to him to have his friends take the boat out on one last trip, in his memory.'

'Impossible.' The young port police man shakes his head.

Lazarus does not argue. 'Is Demosthenes here?' he asks instead.

The port police man straightens his back and a muscle in his jaw tenses.

'The commander is busy,' he says, trying to sound authoritative.

'I doubt it.' Lazarus walks around the port police man's desk and taps with his fingers on the frosted glass panel of a door set into a framework that divides part of the room into a separate office.

'Come!' A gruff voice bellows.

Lazarus lets himself into the smaller office and closes the door behind him. The gruff voice greets him cheerfully. Spiros's attention is taken by the crackle of a radio set on one of the desks. Another man in uniform – well, more of a boy really – sits behind the desk, reading a newspaper.

It is not long before the frosted door opens again, and Lazarus comes out shaking hands with a smiling man in a white shirt.

'Coffee on Thursday, then,' the man in the white shirt says in his gruff voice.

'Absolutely!' Lazarus laughs.

The port police commander, still holding Lazarus's hand, still shaking it, looks out into the room and fixes his gaze on the young port police man they spoke to originally. The boy by the radio surreptitiously slides the newspaper onto his knees, shifting it under the desk, and picks up a pencil.

'These gentlemen will be taking a short trip on George's yacht,' the commander announces in his gruff, booming voice. 'It is not official, because the paperwork is not complete, but let's just say that what we don't know about, we can do nothing about, understood?'

It is not a question. Both the uniformed men nod; the port police commander releases Lazarus's hand, taps his index finger against his own forehead in a kind of salute and retreats back into his office, closing his frosted glass door behind him.

'Right, then.' Lazarus adjusts his trousers, pulling them up by the waistband. 'We are set.' And he marches out, with Takis following and Spiros bringing up the rear.

'Are we going sailing?' Spiros whispers to Takis as they hurry after Lazarus.

'Let's see,' Takis says. He does not sound sure.

Outside on the pavement, Lazarus waits for them to catch up. He seems pleased with himself. 'Well, boys, that went well. So, who amongst George's friends would appreciate this remembrance trip?'

Takis opens his mouth and closes it again.

'I mean, I know he was good friends with Thanasis who keeps the donkeys,' Lazarus says.

'Was he?' Takis sounds surprised.

'And there is Theo, of course. You live in that village over there, right, so you know Theo who runs the *kafenio*.'

'Yes, of course,' Takis says, and Spiros thinks he sounds surprised that George knew Theo too.

'I'll tell you what. I will give the people I think would want to do this for George a call. As for the trip, how does tomorrow at ten sound?'

'Fine,' Takis says, and Lazarus starts to walk away.

'Er, just one other thing …' Takis calls after him.

Lazarus turns and waits.

'Do you know how to sail?'

'You mean you don't?' This seems to amuse the man.

'Well, a bit rusty, perhaps,' Takis lies.

'You'll be fine, it's like riding a bike. Besides, I will be there and Thanasis is a good sailor. I don't think he will miss this trip. See you tomorrow.' And then he continues on his way.

'Why did you tell him you could sail?' Spiros asks as they watch him disappear round the corner.

'I didn't say I could sail. I said I was a bit rusty. I didn't say what I was rusty at,' Takis says defensively.

'But you …' Spiros knows from experience that it is pointless to argue with Takis. He will talk fast and bring in things that have nothing to do with the original question, and soon Spiros will feel confused and Takis will grow smug, and it always ends with Spiros feeling as if he has been made a fool of, so he closes his mouth.

'Well, the sun is going down. I suggest we take the road back to the village, and maybe someone will stop and give us a lift.'

The next morning, Takis wakes Spiros early and they are both in the village square by nine-thirty. If Theo and Thanasis are going to come on the sailing trip, they will each pass through the square on the way to Saros, and maybe they can get a lift. Before long, Theo appears.

'Morning,' he says cheerfully.

He has a bag with him and Spiros hopes there are sandwiches in it, or a loaf of bread at least. His last meal was the chicken dinner with Babis, and he has had nothing since, not even a snack. The chickens had only left one egg this morning, and he boiled it for his mama. If they are to go out on the boat, they could be hours. Maybe he should mention this to Takis, but then what could he do? He has no money for food either.

'Morning,' Takis replies.

Theo and Takis stand facing each other, shifting their weight from foot to foot, as if they are slightly nervous.

'Morning,' calls a chirpy voice. Thanasis the village donkey breeder strides out, marching towards them across the square.

'Are we late?' Another voice calls and Spiros is pleased to see Aleko, who fixes engines and things, with his daughter Eva and a boy about her age, whom he does not know.

'Everyone, this is Giuseppe, Eva's fiancé,' Aleko announces.

'Fiancé, eh?' Thanasis speaks first. 'Well, congratulations, Eva. But no, wait, I should say that to you, young man, as it is you who have struck lucky with such a catch as Eva!' Thanasis seems in a good mood.

'Do we know how many we are waiting for?' Theo asks.

'I think this is it, from what Lazarus said. Do we want to go in my truck?' Aleko says, and he points to his house, back behind the *kafenio*. Spiros is watching Eva, who has a basket covered with a cloth. That must be food – no one would carry anything but food like that, would they?

Once they are all settled in the truck the smell of home baking fills the cab.

'Well, Athena was going to come,' Aleko says as he puts the keys in the ignition, 'but with all the children to take care of she has decided to stay at home.'

'But she has sent this picnic,' Eva adds, and there are murmurs of how kind it is, and what a wonderful way it will be to remember George.

After that no one says much on the way to Saros. At one point Spiros has trouble stifling a yawn, and this sets the others off yawning too. Once they are in Saros, the truck is abandoned by the port police building and, as a group, they chatter as they make their way to the boat. When they arrive at the boat, though, the mood becomes more sombre.

'I'll miss that old goat,' Aleko says.

'He wasn't an old goat – he was a sweet old man, Baba, and I will miss him too. He was very wise in his own way,' Eva says.

'I didn't know you even knew him,' Theo says.

'He came to eat with us sometimes, more and more as he got older. I don't think he took good care of himself,' Eva says as she takes a seat in the cockpit. Her fiancé sits silently by her side.

'He had that leg trouble,' Thanasis says, absentmindedly coiling a rope and looping it round one of the winches. Lazarus is taking in the fenders that hang down on either side, lifting them up over the rail and storing them neatly on the deck.

'He should have had a doctor look at his legs,' he adds.

'He did, didn't he?' Theo does not look as comfortable on board as Thanasis and Lazarus. He joins Eva and her fiancé sitting in the cockpit.

'He had an operation on them and the doctor told him to keep walking, but he said it hurt.' Aleko opens the hatch and disappears down the steps into the bowels of the yacht. Spiros is fascinated, and peers down into the dark but hesitates to follow.

'Sorry, do you want to get past?' Eva says, and she moves to one side, leaving room for him to step past her after her baba.

It is dark and smells of stale cigarettes down below. To one side is a little sink and a little stove, with cupboards above. In the centre is a large table, with padded seats all the way around, and on the opposite side, facing the kitchen area, is another, smaller table, above which is a panel with rows of switches on it.

Aleko flicks a couple of the switches, and red lights come on above each one. There is a brief whirring noise from under the floor, and then it stops. Spiros hesitates to think of the space they are in as a room, because the sides are not square and instead follow the curve of the boat. But other aspects are like a room, such as at the far end, where three doors lead off a narrow corridor, one to the left, one to the right, one straight ahead. Behind him, on either side of the steps he has just come down, are more narrow doors. The place feels magical, a world Spiros has never seen before. Although it is a bit worn and well-used, Spiros can tell that the interior of the boat is what others mean when they say words like luxurious. The walls are all panelled in dark wood, which shine dully in the dim light, and the ceiling is padded with a material that looks like white leather. There are shelves built into many of the surfaces, and little cupboard doors in odd places. Everywhere he looks there are secret hiding places, shelves and cupboards.

'Wow!' he says.

'Well, that's all working,' Aleko says cheerfully, looking at the panel with the lights and switches. 'And I know the engine is good as I overhauled it in the winter. So we are ready to go.'

He squeezes past and skips up the steps. There is a high-pitched whistle and then the engine begins to throb. Down below, the deep booming sound echoes in the small space; it is noisy and just the slightest bit frightening.

'Come and sit with us,' Eva says when Spiros comes up the steps.

He feels a little overwhelmed by the noises he heard in the enclosed space below deck and is glad to be breathing fresh sea air again.

'There's no wind,' Lazarus says, 'so I suggest we motor round the coast to the island of Lakos. There's a little bay on the far side that you can only get to by boat. We can put the anchor down there and go for a swim. It's beautiful, and it was one of George's favourite places to take his clients. I think it would be a very fitting destination.'

Aleko is at the wheel and Thanasis is still coiling ropes and piling them on top of each other on the deck.

'I think a lot of these ropes want ditching, Taki – they look old and you don't want a rope snapping on you when you need it to hold.'

'Yes, quite,' Takis says, and Spiros hears in the tone of his voice that he is bluffing.

'Would you like some gum?' Eva asks him.

'No, thank you.' Spiros looks over at her fiancé, whose hair is a mess of curls, some of which fall over his eyes.

'Pippo is Italian,' Eva says.

'Hi,' Pippo says in English; it reminds Spiros of the American films he likes to watch.

'Hi,' he replies, and Pippo smiles and then looks away, as if that's all that needs to be said, and they are friends now.

Spiros is aware his looks and his size can make people behave in strange ways towards him. He can't do anything about being big and muscular, nor about the fact that his hair will not sit flat to his head and sticks up in places. But it's his face that causes people to react. He knows from looking in the mirror why it bothers people most: he just doesn't look normal. But Pippo didn't react as if Spiros was any different from anyone else. He didn't speak slowly to him, as if he was deaf – he just said 'hi' and carried on sitting. Spiros relaxes and sits back, and watches a seagull far up in the sky.

Aleko the garage man, his daughter Eva and her fiancé Pippo and Takis all take seats in the cockpit as Lazarus stands behind the big wheel, steering. Spiros makes a list of all the people on the boat and brings each face to mind, silently repeating the names. Thanasis is at the front, pressing buttons on the controller to pull the anchor up, the chain clanking in noisily.

They motor past the island fort, out of the bay and along the coast. The yacht moves smoothly through the water, which is calm, oily, and the only waves are those made by the passage of the boat, fanning out behind them far into the distance. The early morning sunlight dances off the wavelets, and the land slides by on one side.

Spiros can hardly sit still, he is so excited. He is on a yacht! His yacht … well, his and Takis's. It's odd to see the town from this angle, and he is riveted as they glide by – there's the town beach, with only a few people on it at this time of the morning, like ants from this distance. Beyond the beach the coastline is rocky, falling steeply from the path that leads south away from the town. Pine trees cling to the slopes, and here and there are tiny inlets, some with little sandy beaches, completely inaccessible from the land, but his to discover now that he has his own boat! The others talk quietly, reminiscing about George, commenting on the novelty of the experience. It seems no one spends much time on the water except Lazarus, who steers with one hand casually resting on the wheel, his eyes half closed against the bright sun. Spiros stands, takes a moment to adjust to the slight motion of the boat, shifting his weight from foot to foot.

'Is it okay if I go to the front?' he asks Takis, pointing in the direction they are travelling.

'Hold on,' says Lazarus, and Takis adds, 'Don't fall in!' and the others laugh, but not unkindly, and Spiros steps up onto the deck and makes his way to the very front.

He grips the guard rail all the way, although there is really no need; there is still only the lightest of breezes, and the deck of the yacht is only rocking ever so gently. At the very front of the yacht is a little wooden seat and below it is a hatch that covers the anchor and chain. Perched on this seat, Spiros is suspended out over the water, as if he is a figurehead on one of the pirate ships that he has seen pictures of. Sitting here, it feels as if he is flying, skimming across the waves like the seagulls. He looks down to where the bows of the boat are slicing the calm surface, sending up a curl of white water on either side, breaking the surface into a million droplets. He closes his eyes and feels the breeze against his face. He looks back to the rear of the boat where the others are sitting. Friends, on an adventure together. And now that the boat is theirs – who knows, perhaps there will be many days like this, and maybe they will even be able to take tourists out and be paid for it, like George was.

Up ahead, the island is growing bigger, and Spiros tries to see the bay that they are heading for, the one Lazarus described. When they get there they will have a picnic, and a swim. Spiros's stomach rumbles. The wind is starting to get up, just a little, and the surface of the water is suddenly split into tiny shimmering diamonds, each reflecting the sun, which is inching higher into the sky. It is hot and he wipes his forehead with his forearm. Perhaps he should have brought a hat.

Spiros stands and makes his way back to the cockpit and sits with his friends.

'Another ten minutes or so.' Lazarus has taken over steering from Aleko. 'Can someone get the anchor?'

No one else moves, and Spiros is on his feet again, hurrying back to the bows.

'Lift the lid of the box in the floor there,' Lazarus calls. 'Yes, that's it. Do you see the control button?'

Spiros finds the controller and holds it up over his head, waving it so Lazarus can see.

'That's it,' Lazarus says, smiling encouragingly. 'I'll let you know when to drop the anchor.'

This is even more exciting than he imagined. They are approaching the island quite quickly now, and as they round the next headland the bay opens out to reveal a wide sweep of fine white sand, with pine trees and rocks behind. There are no other boats, no people, and the sea is a clear emerald blue. Lazarus slows the boat, and the engine noise drops. The boat edges deeper into the bay, approaching the shore, and Spiros looks down into the clear water. They are sheltered from the breeze here and the sea is absolutely calm. He can see all the way to the bottom: rocks, sand, and clumps of weed waving in the currents, with shoals of fish darting here and there.

'Right, here will do,' Lazarus calls, and Spiros hurries to lift the heavy anchor, dropping it off the front and then pressing the button on the controller to let the chain run out. He watches the anchor as it sinks into the water, all the way to the bottom, lifting a small cloud of sand as it settles. The chain runs out, lying in a snaky line along the bottom, and Lazarus cuts the engine. The silence is almost total, and as Spiros looks around at the bay they are moored in, he thinks it is one of the most perfect places he has ever seen.

Thanasis has come up to the front and stands next to him, looking down onto the water.

'Good job,' he says.

'Pippo and I are going for a swim,' Eva announces.

Theo just strips off his T-shirt and dives off the edge of the boat without a word, splashing into the water. They watch him swim a few strokes under the surface and then he emerges, laughing. Flicking his hair out of his eyes, he lazily rolls over, and then, as if it is the easiest thing in the world, he begins to swim as fast as a fish towards the beach.

'Are you going in?' Takis asks Lazarus.

'I am like George, never learnt to swim,' he says, and he leaves his place by the wheel to take a seat in the cockpit.

'Sailors never used to learn to swim, did they, because it was said that if they fell in it would stretch out their death,' Thanasis says, looking out towards the island.

'That was George's thinking too,' Lazarus says.

Theo is on the beach now, and Eva and Giuseppe are halfway across. Spiros wonders whether he could make it to the island, but decides he will wait; he might swim later.

'Not many boats sleep eight,' Thanasis muses.

'Eight?' Takis repeats.

'Didn't you know? You must have been down below and checked out the rooms?' Thanasis says in a lazy voice. His eyes are closed and his head lolls with the gentle rocking of the boat.

'Two double cabins aft and a shower and toilet, and another two cabins up front. And a second bathroom.' Lazarus kicks his shoes off and puts his feet up on the seat opposite. He has a hole in the toe of one sock.

'Yup, George has passed you on a gold mine,' says Thanasis lazily.

'Actually, if you use the seats in the saloon as beds, which is how they were designed, then she sleeps ten.' Lazarus sounds like he is half asleep already.

'Ten!' Takis repeats. He sounds far from sleep and is on his feet and making his way down below. Spiros follows, keen to see the little beds and the little toilets. It sounds like a doll's house.

The first door he tries opens to reveal a toilet that is so small he would struggle to get in and turn around. There is a showerhead mounted on the wall behind the door, and it is clear that the whole room is the shower – you could close the toilet lid and use it as a seat as you washed. Even so, it is a very tight space. There are shelves built in and a first-aid box attached to the wall. The soap is in a bottle with a press-top dispenser, and a towel hangs on the door. The floor is a wooden latticework that allows the shower water to drain away.

The next door leads into a cabin. The bed takes up the whole space, and it is shaped to fit the walls that curve in, so that the bed is wide at the end nearest the door and gets narrower towards the back of the boat. If there were two people in there, their feet would get tangled up! It looks comfortable, though, and cleaner than the saloon.

Takis comes out of the cabin at the front of the boat.

'This will be like printing money, Spiro,' he says. 'When we've learnt to sail, this will be the life, taking people to this bay, letting them swim, sailing them back again, back and forth every day and making a fortune.'

Spiros grins. 'Can we sleep on board?'

'You can when we are doing that.'

After an hour or so, the swimmers return, invigorated, with the sea in their eyes. Lazarus opens out a little folding table and the food is spread out. Spiros is starving but he tries really hard not to eat too quickly. Eva keeps asking if he wants more, and when he says no, she doesn't believe him and gives him more anyway.

'I have brothers,' she says, and he eats all she gives him, and then he feels so full he wonders if it would be more comfortable if he loosened his trousers. He doesn't because Eva is there.

'Well, I think George would have enjoyed this,' Eva says as she starts scrunching up the aluminium foil and putting lids on Tupperware boxes.

'I think he would be happy to think the boat is carrying on without him,' Thanasis says.

'Yes, and so it should,' Lazarus agrees.

'And why not? You have everything you need. This vessel must be big enough to give you both an income,' Theo says.

'It is the gift of a lifetime,' Giuseppe says, and they all laugh at his Greek, but not unkindly. 'You laugh, eh? But you won't laugh when our friends here have this boat

42

filled with tourists in the summer.' He grins and wags a finger comically.

'Well,' says Lazarus finally, 'we'll have a good sail back.' He points out to the sea, where small whitecaps have started to appear, showing that the wind has come up.

'That's a thermal wind,' he adds, 'and it will take us back to Saros. We can use the sails – I bet you'll all like that! Once we get going, Spiro, you should have a go at steering.'

Spiros stands, ready to lift the anchor again, ready for anything. He has never felt so good.

Chapter 4

'So you made it back in one piece, then?' The young port police man looks a little surprised to see them and he glances at the door to the police commander's office, hesitant to disturb him, perhaps.

'Yes, with no problems.'

Takis sounds so confident, as if it was he who fixed the engine when it wouldn't start in the bay after lunch. Spiros rubs his eye, which is twitching at the memory. When it happened, Takis's face turned white, and Pippo put his arm around Eva, but Aleko smiled, rolled up his sleeves and disappeared below deck.

'Hey, Taki, you want to see this,' he called up, and Spiros followed Takis down the steps to have a look. The engine was housed in the space behind the steps, and Aleko had pulled them out so he could get at it, and they wobbled alarmingly as Spiros climbed down them.

'Nothing serious,' Aleko said as Takis crouched beside him, peering into the dark space behind the treads. The engine was big and mysterious, the dark matt metal poking up between the floorboards, hot and smelling of burnt motor oil.

'See that hose,' Aleko said to Takis, 'well, that pulls in seawater to cool the engine. The connection here was loose, and not only was there no water getting to the engine but the seawater was coming in. There's already ten centimetres in the bottom of the boat here, and if I hadn't spotted it, well …. You'll learn many things if you keep the boat on, but this one is worth knowing right now, as it could sink you.'

He finished his lesson with a wink and Spiros was not sure if the bit about sinking had been a joke.

'Was that why it wouldn't start?' Takis asked.

'Oh no,' said Aleko, 'it was just a loose connection on the starter motor. But it's for the best, really, or we wouldn't have noticed this loose hose. Maybe not till it was too late.'

Once they were underway, Lazarus was as good as his word and showed Spiros how to steer the boat. It felt frightening to do so, but only for a minute.

'You're a natural,' Lazarus said, and this gave him confidence. Spiros steered all the way back to Saros, and the others referred to him as the captain, except for Takis. Spiros had never felt such unbridled joy.

When they reached the port Lazarus took over again, saying he needed Spiros to deal with the anchor. Lazarus steered the boat in reverse towards the harbour wall and called out to him to drop the anchor when they were still some way out from the pier. Takis and Thanasis stood at the rear, each with a coil of rope, ready to leap out onto the hard when they got close enough.

'Drop the anchor when I tell you', Lazarus said, 'and then press the button to let the chain out, quickly enough so that it doesn't go taut and stop the boat, but not too fast or it will sit in a big heap on the bottom.'

But the chain had got stuck over the roller; Spiros reached down to free it, but Lazarus screamed at him to stop.

'Don't put your fingers near it!' Lazarus shouted, and Theo abandoned his rope and rushed to Spiros in alarm. He took the controller away for a moment and the winch motor stopped, and then Theo stood on the chain, putting his full weight on it to free it. He did give the controller back, though, so Spiros got to finish the job with the big red button and the clanking chain.

Spiros's grin returns at the memory.

'So, what can I do for you?' the port police man asks.

'I wish to continue the yacht business,' Takis says, his chest all puffed out.

'And what does that have to do with me?' the man enquires.

This seems to confuse Takis, just for a second.

'Well, Lazarus says there will be things we need to clear with you. We'll need passenger forms or something, and I'll need a skipper's licence.'

'I think perhaps you need to get the boat in your name first,' the port police man says, 'then go get your skipper's licence, and after that you can come to us.'

'So how do I get a skipper's licence?'

The uniformed man puts his hands on the desk and looks down. He takes a deep slow breath and lets it out before he looks up again.

'There's a school in Athens. I don't have the number, but ask anyone in the marina there for Lakis. He runs an offshore sailing school. But go and see your lawyer first. Get the papers sorted out and then think about licences.'

He turns away from Takis and starts to shuffle papers on top of a metal filing cabinet. The man at the radio releases a short snigger. A seagull flies past the window and lets out a raucous cry.

'Okay,' Takis persists, 'so, supposing the boat is in my name, and I have a licence. What next?' He sounds exasperated. The port police man continues walking his fingers through the files in the cabinet; he doesn't turn to look at Takis. His voice is flat, uninterested.

'After that, go see your accountant. Register as a business. Then come back to us, and bring your insurance certificate. Get the life raft inspected, and the radio, and bring those certificates too …'

Needless to say, Takis is in a bad mood as they begin the walk home. Spiros is not too happy either. If they had not wasted their time going to the port police they could have got a lift back to the village with Aleko in his big truck. His wife, Athena, might even have invited them for dinner. Now they have to walk back and they still have no money and no food at home.

He should have tried for the job herding Mitsos's goats when he had the chance. But then again, if he had done that he would not have sailed today, and that was an experience he will not forget for a long time. Life seems to be full of these hard choices; sometimes it is easier to simply let Takis tell him what to do.

'It's going to cost,' Takis says. 'First of all the skipper's licence will cost, that's for sure, and all those certificates to satisfy the port police! Thanasis says we need new ropes and I think he is right, and they will cost. I also think we need smart new fenders to make the yacht look good, which means more money. The only thing we can do that doesn't take money is scrub the decks.'

Spiros knows exactly who Takis has in mind to scrub the decks. But the moment of resentment passes quickly; after all, it is his deck too, and it's a way in which he can be helpful! It's the money he can't help with.

'Maybe we can get someone to go in with us who has money?' he suggests.

'You know,' says Takis, a slow smile creeping onto his lips, 'that's not such a bad idea. They can pay everything up front and then we pay them back with a little on top when the boat is working.'

'Yacht,' Spiros says.

'When we get back, we should see Babis. He will tell us everything we need to do and he's a rich man. He wouldn't miss a handful of money to start us off.'

Takis quickens his pace and Spiros lengthens his stride to keep up.

'Hello, come in,' Babis greets them warmly.

But getting into his house is not an easy affair. Some coats have fallen from the back of the door and are now wedged under it, and no amount of shoving will open it more, and Babis seems reluctant to go to the trouble of closing it, hanging up the jackets and opening it again.

'Can you squeeze in?' he says, and he leaves them to manage as best they can.

His house is cluttered. Clothes are strewn on most items of furniture, and dirty dishes are liberally scattered about the room. Babis leads them through the messy sitting room to the kitchen, where plates are piled high in the sink and on the work surfaces and there is a smell of cabbage. The table is relatively clear; some paperwork covers a portion of it and it looks as if they have interrupted his work.

'So, what can I do for you boys?' He sits on the one chair that does not have things piled on it.

'I was just wondering,' Takis starts, and then he looks at Spiros – 'or rather, *we* were just wondering what we have to do to run the boat like George did?'

'Oh, right, yes, good idea. You'd make more money long term than if you sold it, and it would give you boys a permanent job. Yes, I can see your logic. Well, you will have to register as a business, obviously.'

He picks up the pen and taps it against the papers. Dark circles of sweat under his arms mar his otherwise pristine white shirt.

'Once you have done that you will need to start paying TEBE immediately, I'm afraid, and it's not cheap.' He looks at Spiros as he delivers this news.

Spiros shakes his head. Takis nods and tuts, as if this expense is nothing more than he expected.

'Speak to Drakakis, George's accountant, and he will help you register the boat as a business, and tell you what papers you need to take to the tax office.'

Takis's face has lost a little colour. He steps a little closer to the table, towards Babis.

'Here's the thing, Babi. I – we – think the boat could be a gold mine, and I am younger than George was, and Spiros here is just a pup ... We have the energy and I know we could make it work, but it's going to take some money to start us off.'

Babis is looking down at his papers as the word 'money' is spoken. He looks like he might have stopped listening, and he is reading the top sheet of printed paper on his kitchen table.

Takis persists. 'But I would be happy to pay anyone who would be willing to lend us enough to get started – let's say, ten per cent interest?'

Takis waits for Babis to respond.

'Or even twenty per cent,' he adds, when Babis does not look up. His voice has a quiver in it. 'In fact, I would be happy to give that person half as much back as well as their investment – now you cannot say fairer than that, can you?'

He slaps the tabletop with the flat of his hand and Babis's papers jump.

Spiros watches the lawyer's face, but he cannot tell if he was even listening.

'Here's what to do, boys,' Babis announces finally, putting his pen down and lacing his fingers together. With his elbows on the table, he rests his chin lightly on his hands.

'Go to George's accountant, make a list of all the costs – all of them, mind – and then come back and let's see, shall we?'

He unlaces his fingers, folds his arms and sits back in his chair. The discussion is closed. Spiros gets ready to leave.

'Have you eaten?' Takis asks Babis as he stands.

'Are you offering?' Babis counters.

Takis pulls a strange face, a mix of amusement, apology and anger.

'Come on, Spiro,' he says with a bit of a growl. Babis doesn't even get up from his chair as they turn to leave. On the way out, Spiros takes the time to hang the jackets on the hook on the back of the door, but as he pulls the door shut he hears them fall again.

'So is he going to help us?' he asks, once they are outside.

Takis does not answer, and he stamps off in the direction of home. That's not good. If they go home now that means trying to get to sleep on an empty stomach.

'Be up tomorrow bright and early,' is all he says when they reach his front door.

Spiros puts his arm across his stomach and wonders whether his mama will be asleep, and if not, whether she will have something to eat left over. But no light shows between her shutters or under her door, and when he presses his ear against the wood he can hear her gently snoring.

The cockerel crows before it is light and Spiros rubs his eyes, pulls on yesterday's trousers and goes outside to wait for Takis. He checks the hens but there are no eggs in their little hut, and so he reminds himself, again, that he must make some time to find out where they are laying. An egg for his breakfast would be nice. But he will not search just now; he will wake up a little first. He rubs his eyes and sits on the doorstep. The birds all around are twittering their morning chorus, and up in the hill behind his house a donkey brays, sucking in its dismay and heaving out its loneliness. He loves donkeys. Almost as much as goats. If he could have a perfect job it would be working for Thanasis who breeds donkeys, and at some point each day herding Mitsos's goats. What a wonderful life that would be.

The cockerel crows again. And again. By the time Takis opens his door and comes out stretching and yawning, it is quite light.

'Morning.' Spiros feels good after listening to the birds and the donkey and the cockerel and the cicadas, and his sleepiness is forgotten.

Takis grunts at him and returns indoors. Spiros sits and listens to the sounds of the morning, letting the first rays of the sun warm his face, and when Takis appears again, his face pink and a little shiny, water still dripping from his chin, they walk side by side down to the village square.

This early in the morning there are several cars around, some paused by the kiosk, and a couple with the engines running by the tiny sandwich shop opposite Stella's eatery, which has yet to open. Another car is stationary by the corner shop, with its driver's-side door open. Takis does not hesitate: when the driver comes out of the shop with a blue plastic bag, bread poking out of the top, he asks for a lift to Saros town and motions Spiros to get in the back.

Not being exactly sure where George's accountant's office is, they get out by the harbour and wander around asking for directions. Eventually they are directed to a white plastic door in the side of an old, tall building, which gives access to an office divided down the middle by a bamboo screen. On the other side of the screen, with his back to the window, is a man, head bent over his desk, wearing a jumper despite the heat.

'Ahem.' Takis makes a false coughing sound.

'Sit.' The man does not look up and so they sit either side of a small table stacked with men's fashion magazines, a bowl of wrapped sweets on the top. Their backs are to the bamboo screen. Spiros takes a sweet, and in the silence he unwraps it and sucks on it. There's no bin so he puts the wrapper back in the dish. The sweet is horrible, and tastes like perfume. Maybe he could rewrap it, but then what would he do with it? He couldn't put it back with the other sweets. He decides the best option is to swallow it whole. With a gulp it is gone and he selects a second sweet, a different colour, to take the taste of the first away.

'Right, how can I help you?' Drakakis says finally, looking up at them. His jumper has been knitted thicker around the neck and the collar crosses over at the front. The jumper is somehow at odds with his age and occupation. He seems like a serious, solid man, perhaps in his early fifties, and the jumper is trendy; the two do not seem to fit. His hair is darker than Takis's, but there is less of it, and it is combed over his head in the same way as Takis's. This, too, seems at odds with the way he is dressed.

'We inherited George's yacht.' Takis puts a hand on each of his knees and smiles, as if waiting to be congratulated.

'Ah, dear,' Drakakis the accountant says.

'It is a gold mine, isn't it?' Takis says, still smiling, but not quite so broadly as before.

'What month are we in?' the accountant asks. Takis frowns. There is a calendar on the wall and it seems an odd question.

'Beginning of July?' he says cautiously.

'So it's summer.' Drakakis still has one eye on the papers in front of him, and he makes the occasional tick or cross at the end of the printed lines, working down the sheet.

'Ye-e-es …'

Drakakis looks at Takis and points with his pen over his shoulder to the darkened glass window. 'Well, take a look. It's summer, we live in a pretty town full of history, by the sea, and how many tourists do you see?'

Spiros watches Takis's Adam's apple bob as he absorbs this comment.

'Oh, well, of course we would advertise,' Takis counters.

'You will advertise,' Drakakis repeats. 'Where? The Netherlands, Spain, England, America? Where are you going to bring these tourists from?'

'Athens,' Takis says, but he doesn't sound sure. 'And Stella's hotel.'

'Well, that's a good thought. If you can follow that line of thinking and find a way to get in touch with whoever brings the tourists to Stella's hotel, then maybe they can add you to their list of attractions, but it's an expensive business.'

He takes a white sheet of paper and as he talks he writes down numbers.

'There are the skipper's fees, of course. I take it neither of you has a licence, and I have no idea how much those cost these days. I took mine way back when we still reckoned in drachmas.'

He writes on the sheet of paper the word *Licence* and puts a question mark next to it.

'Then the day-to-day running costs – well, they're not too bad. There are the mooring fees' – he writes the words and scribbles a figure – 'and water and diesel.'

Two more numbers go on the list.

'You'll need to keep some cash in reserve so you can take the boat out of the water every two years to clean and inspect the bottom.'

Another number.

'Sails need replacing every once in a while.'

This gets another question mark.

'The toilets get blocked and broken because you will find that tourists don't care as much as you do about the pumps.'

Another question mark.

'The engine servicing will need to be written up in your service log, and you need to keep an eye on your instruments – you don't want your GPS, your wind meter or your depth gauge going wrong, and of course your radio needs a service every year as it's a safety issue. Does it have an automatic pilot? I can't remember. That can be expensive.'

Drakakis stops for breath.

'You're a skipper – you have a boat?' Takis asks.

'I *was* a skipper and I *had* a boat. It was a pot to pour money into. Expensive business, boats, very little return.'

He points at a framed photo, on the wall, of what looks like an advert for a boat. The shot has been taken side-on to show the vessel's lines to their best advantage, and standing on the bow is a man with his hands in his pockets, looking as if he does not have a care in the world. It is only the jumper, similar to the one the accountant is wearing, that identifies the man in the picture as Drakakis. Presumably the picture was taken a few years back, as the man in the photo has considerably more hair.

'So …' The accountant taps on the page of numbers with his pen. 'Add this up.'

The pen scratches out what looks like a big number to Spiros.

'And George earned this much …' – the pen flicks and makes a mark here and there as Drakakis calculates – 'so you will need to get ten people to take a day's sail with you, at sixty euros per head, so that will mean you need the boat at half capacity for this many days a year to just break even.'

He appears to have enjoyed the challenge of adding up the numbers, but the reality of the result makes Takis gasp.

'Although, that is not so many days out of the year if we have her working at full capacity,' Takis reasons.

'In all the years I have been doing George's accounts, I've only known him to have a full boat half a dozen times. If he was half full he would consider that a good day. And of course, that means no days off over the summer – you simply couldn't afford to.'

'Okay, so we could break even, and then any extra days will put some money in our pockets, if we work hard, but ...' Takis starts to chuckle, and he slaps his hands together and rubs them. 'Think of all the tourist girls that I – I mean, we – will spend day after day with.' He grins broadly at Drakakis.

'You want families,' Drakakis says flatly. 'Families come in sets, usually four. Two families and you have reached a good capacity. Also, they have the money. Tourist girls come in twos and they are usually broke. You need four pairs of tourist girls to equal two families, which means twice the work to find them and get them to sign up.'

Takis face loses its look of glee.

'Well, Saros isn't Mykonos, is it?' Drakakis shrugs.

Spiros takes another sweet as they leave, being careful to choose one of the yellow ones. Takis is glum and agitated at the same time.

'Does this means we are picking oranges and olives again this coming winter? Shall I ask Mitsos if I can herd his goats?' Spiros asks.

'We must be able to think of something better than that. We still have the yacht, right?' Takis retorts.

Chapter 5

'We cannot go in there, we have no money.'

Spiros grabs Takis's sleeve as he heads towards Theo's *kafenio* after they finally arrive back at the village square.

'I tell you what, I'm sick of all this walking back and forth to Saros. How many people in this village have a yacht? One! Me! I should be living a life of luxury, not going hungry and unable to afford a coffee after such a walk.'

'But we haven't got any money, so how will you pay Theo?' Spiros lets go of Takis's sleeve.

'He didn't pay me for the trip on the boat, did he?' Takis retorts.

Spiros cannot fault this logic but somehow the two seem different. If he could take a moment, he feels, he could work out why the two are not the same, but Takis is in no mood to wait and he is already up the steps and into the *kafenio*, leaving Spiros to chase after him.

'Hey, you two.' Theo saunters over.

The place is fairly full – it's that time of the evening – and as Spiros looks around he recognises all the faces, having worked for most of them at one time or another. A pair of farmers at the next table nod at Spiros; he has worked for them both, picking oranges, harvesting olives, planting young saplings and clearing orchard after orchard of stones.

Many of the older men were his baba's friends. Spiros looks around for his baba, but of course he is not here, will never be here again. At moments like these, seeing all his baba's friends together, the years disappear and he expects him to be alive again and sitting in his place amongst them. He looks to Takis to ground himself in reality again.

Takis's parents have been dead for many years. Takis is not as old as Spiros's baba was when he died, but he is old enough to have been at school with some of the older farmers here tonight.

'Did you enjoy the jaunt in the boat?' Takis asks Theo, who stands waiting to take their order.

'It was a good way to remember George.'

Theo allows a moment's pause and then asks, 'Coffee, ouzo?' The *kafenio* actually serves a variety of drinks, but Spiros has rarely seen the farmers drink anything but ouzo or coffee.

'Two ouzos, Theo. I am feeling a little sad about George, and an ouzo would be soothing to the soul.' Takis nods his head slowly and his bottom lip quivers. Theo mirrors the nodding of the head, pats him on the shoulder and then trots away to fulfil the order.

'I'm sorry you are sad, Taki.' Spiros puts a concerned hand on his friend's shoulder.

'Well, a little comforting ouzo will help while we figure out what to do.'

All traces of sadness seem to have gone now Theo has left.

'So, we have a boat.' Takis makes this firm statement as if it is the start of an announcement.

'Yacht.'

'Boat, yacht, whatever. It is worth money, right?'

'Right.'

'Ah, thank you, Theo.'

Theo places two tall glasses full of ice on the table and then pours liberally from an ouzo bottle. Takis raises the first glass.

'To George and his yacht,' he says, and as Theo finishes pouring the second, Takis chinks his tumbler against the bottle and says quietly, 'and the bottle for George, if you like.'

Spiros is not sure what this is intended to mean, and it seems that Theo is confused too, as he hesitates and a little crease appears on his brow.

Takis taps the table with his glass and looks at Theo, who stands holding the bottle.

'For George,' Takis says again, and Theo's eyebrows don't seem sure whether to frown or not. He puts the bottle on the table, which draws a smile from Takis, and when Theo walks away he leaves the bottle between them.

'Cheers,' Takis says to Spiros.

'But I don't like ouzo.'

'It's aniseed. Have you ever really tried it?'

'Once, ages ago.'

'Well, you are a man who owns a yacht now, so welcome to the high life.'

He motions for Spiros to take up his glass. The first tiny sip tastes nice, but the second, bigger sip burns his throat. The third has a curious effect, as if someone has wiped out the inside of his head with a clean cloth and all his worries have gone with the dirt. He likes that, so he takes another gulp.

'So, we need money to make it work for us, and I am almost positive that Babis will not be willing to lend us as much as Drakakis reckons we'll need.'

Spiros knows this should make him sad and worried but for some reason he wants to laugh – laugh and drink more ouzo. He puts a hand over his mouth to keep the giggles in.

'But the boat is worth money, so we can sell it, right?'

This does make Spiros sad. He wants to sail again, visit the bay at the back of the little island, maybe even swim next time. Take hold of the wheel and steer the ship, the wind in his face, the seagulls screeching high above the taut, white sails.

'But,' Takis continues before he can object, 'the boat looks bad. I mean, the worn ropes, the paint scuffed off the fenders, the worn cushions in the saloon … The covers of those need replacing, at least. That is all money.'

He takes a long drink. Spiros has finished his ouzo and he pours himself another. He can feel Takis looking at him as he does this, but for some reason he does not care just now what Takis thinks. The remaining ice in his glass turns the clear liquid opaque as he pours, which distracts him and makes him forget to stop pouring. By the time he does stop, his glass is very full and he wonders if he should pour some back. But he can't really; the neck of the

62

bottle is too narrow, and he would make a mess. Best just drink slowly; he does not have to finish it all.

'Hm,' Takis muses, looking down at his feet. He seems to be thinking hard.

Spiros is surprised to find that he finishes his second glass without any difficulty, and Theo comes over with a bowl of ice and spoons cubes into both their glasses. He goes back to his counter and returns again with a little *meze* of olives and salami, two hunks of bread and a sliced tomato.

'Eat a little,' he encourages Spiros, 'or the ouzo will go to your head.' And with a glance at Takis, who is still deep in thought, he leaves them alone again.

Spiros hungrily polishes off the food and then feels bad that he did not leave any for Takis.

'Okay!' Takis exclaims suddenly, as Spiros is swallowing the last mouthful. 'I have it!'

'Have what?'

'I have the way to make most money for absolutely no outlay.'

'Outlay?'

'Spending.'

'Oh. How?' He is not as interested as he was. Takis, from certain angles, seems to be two people: an outline, and a shadow next to him. If he closes one eye, the shadow Takis is gone. This amuses him, and he closes first one eye and then the other, making Takis leap from side to side. But after a couple of minutes this makes him feel dizzy so he stops.

His stomach feels a little better with some food in it, but he is beginning to realise that his head has had a lot of ouzo. He looks out of the window in an attempt to focus on something, to sober himself up a little.

The *kafenio* has floor-to-ceiling windows on two sides and he amuses himself watching people coming and going from the corner shop and the kiosk in the centre of the square. Without realising it, he is playing a game, trying to guess who will go to the corner shop, who will visit the kiosk, and who will go to both. The kiosk does not sell eggs, for example, and the corner shop does not stock German beers. There are bound to be other things, too, that someone might want and can only get by visiting both places. It's entertaining to try to guess what each person has bought.

It feels like he has been playing this game for hours by the time Takis leans towards him and whispers in his ear.

'We sink it.'

'What?' Spiros thinks he must have misheard, or that he has lost the thread of the conversation. Are they still talking about the yacht?

'We sink the boat and we get the insurance money. Insurance always covers more than the item is worth, so if we sink it we don't need to do any of the repairs to make it look good. We just sink it, claim the money, and then if we still want a boat we can buy a new one. Or if the insurance just buys us a boat instead of giving us the money it will be new, no repairs needed.'

'Really?' Spiros tries to understand. He knows that if there is a frost the farmers sometimes claim compensation for the oranges that have fallen to the ground and rotted. He can understand that; it is like a bet. The insurance company bets that the oranges won't fall, and the farmers bet that they will. Whoever is right gets the money. So is insurance on the boat like that? They bet it will sink and the insurance company bets it won't. But then they make it sink anyway? It sounds wrong.

'It's a good plan, eh?' Takis enthuses.

'I don't like the idea of sinking George's boat.'

'Yacht. And it's not George's any more. It's ours now. And anyway, he was always complaining about how much his insurance cost and how he had never made a claim in all the years he had her. So, in a way, this is also justice for George.'

He pours two full glasses of ouzo and Spiros is slightly surprised to see how empty the bottle has become. He is not sure how he did not notice before, and he is definitely sure he should not drink any more. Looking around the *kafenio*, he realises that it is much later than he thought. Time appears to be running more quickly than normal and the place is starting to empty. He had not even noticed that, as he was watching the people going from the corner shop to the kiosk, the light in the square came on; the moon, too, is now illuminating the rooftops with its silver glow. Have they been sitting here in silence for hours? Have they been talking and he hasn't really been listening?

He picks up his ouzo glass and guides it unsteadily to his lips. He seems to spend so much energy being hypervigilant usually, trying to understand the world around him, that it is a relief to have been so relaxed that hours have gone by without him even noticing.

'So it's agreed,' Takis says.

'What's agreed?' Spiros yawns.

'We sink the boat. Come on, there are a few things we need at my house.'

The little bit of ouzo at the bottom of the bottle calls to Spiros but Takis has hold of his arm and is pulling him down the three steps out of the *kafenio*. He glances back at the bottle to see Theo standing in the middle of the room with his hands on his hips, shaking his head as he watches them stagger across the square. There are only a couple of farmers in there now.

'We should have paid Theo,' Spiros says but his mouth doesn't seem to be working properly and it sounds more like 'Mesud've paythio'. It makes him giggle. Takis is still pulling at him.

'*Yeia sou*, Babi!' he calls as they pass the lawyer's door.

'Shh,' Takis commands as they head towards his house.

Takis keeps his tools in a box in the cupboard under the kitchen sink. He takes it out and dumps it on the kitchen table. Inside are balls of tangled string, used bits of sandpaper, a small plastic bag of mismatched screws. There is a soft-headed hammer and Spiros wonders if Takis has a box of rubber nails in there somewhere. The thought makes him laugh out loud.

'There it is.' Eventually, Takis pulls out an adjustable spanner. 'Spiro, wake up.'

'I am no sleep,' he slurs.

'You were slumped on the table, your eyes were closed and you were snoring.'

'I wasnnnn … snoring.' His head does not seem to want to stay upright. He replaces it on the tabletop and closes his eyes.

'Come on,' Takis insists.

The chair is shaking; it's as if the whole ground is moving, but then, as his arm is pulled and he finds his feet, he understands it is Takis's doing.

'You are being an earthquake!' He laughs. He is upright now but his eyes do not want to open. 'I think I will just go up to bed.'

He heads for where his bedroom would be if he were in his own house, but Takis's house is almost a mirror image and his staggering steps take him to the larder.

'My rooms have been stolen!' he says, somewhat horrified, but also finding it funny that there is a tin of wood polish where the end of his bed should be. He stares at it, unsure what to do next.

'Spiro!' Takis's voice is harsh. 'Stop messing about and come on.'

'Where am I coming?'

'I have told you – to sink the boat.'

'Who's going to sink her? They can't do that. I love that boat! George will be very upset.'

'Listen,' Takis's face is very close to his. 'We agreed – to get a new boat that needs no work, to get back all that George has paid to the insurance company all these years, we would sink the boat and claim his money. Now will you come on!'

'Oh, so we are getting George's money back?'

'Yes, George's money, but keep your voice down, it's a secret.'

Spiros shuffles after Takis as he heads out of the door.

'Oh yessss … a shecret. Shhhh.' He stops, puts his finger to his mouth and looks around to make sure no one has heard. He does not remember deciding to come outside. 'Where are we going?'

Takis does not answer, but he takes a firm hold of Spiros's arm and leads him down to the square, where he opens the door of an old truck parked on the corner.

'This is Mitsos's truck! What are you doing with Mitsos's truck?'

'Will you keep your voice down? I'm borrowing it!'

'Have you arshk … arstt … ashhhh … Does he know?'

'Would you want him to wake *you* in the middle of the night to ask if he could borrow your truck?'

Spiros frowns as deeply as he can to think about this.

'But I don't have a truck …'

'Get in,' Takis commands, and like magic he produces keys from behind the sun visor and starts the engine.

'That's a good trick, do another one.'

Spiros looks around the cabin of the truck. He either wants a pillow, or if that is not available he would settle for another shot of ouzo. The truck starts to jiggle as it rumbles out of the square and he grips the door handle and the edge of the seat. Takis is sitting forward in his seat, his face very close to the windscreen, peering through the glass. Only when they are out of the village does he put the headlights on and sit back.

'Maybe this is a dream,' Spiros mutters to himself.

The jolting of the truck is far from comfortable but he leans his head back and closes his eyes anyway. The dream will soon be over and he will find himself in his bed. Actually, he will get up in a minute and go to the bathroom. In a minute. First he will sleep a little more … But the need becomes more pressing. He cannot hang on much longer.

The dream of being in a truck fades and all becomes still. He must get up and use the bathroom or he will have an accident.

'Come on.' Takis is in his dream now, holding the door to the bathroom open for him.

Spiros steps out of bed, but the floor is further away than he thought. He nearly falls but then he doesn't; he stands by the toilet and to his utter relief …

'What on earth are you doing!' Takis's shriek and a hard slap to his arm bring him to his senses. 'You disgusting runt.'

Takis is shaking his trouser leg and with a blinding and horrifying flash Spiros becomes aware of what has happened.

'Oh sorry, I was dreaming.'

He reaches to do something about Takis's wet trousers but then hesitates before he touches them. What can he do? Takis is stamping his foot as if this will dry his trousers, muttering very harsh swear words.

Spiros feels a little bit afraid. He looks around and is shocked to find they are at the far end of Saros harbour, in the shadows of a parked truck.

'I cannot believe you did that …! Come on,' Takis demands in a hushed but angry voice and, crouching low to the ground, he starts to run between cars and palm trees along the harbourfront.

It looks like a fun game so Spiros follows him, bending low and moving through the shadows. He bumps into several of the cars, and he snags his shirt on the spiky branch of a palm tree. At one point he spots a cat asleep on the seat of a motorbike and he stops to pet the creature, but as his hand touches its fur it wakes with a start and leaps down to run away.

When they are on the pier opposite the yacht, Takis stops, ducks behind a wheelie bin and looks around him.

'Right, you go first and then I will come. Go straight down below, though – don't stay on deck,' he orders Spiros. 'Ready? Go!'

He pushes Spiros in his back and Spiros runs to the boat, weaving his way across the gangplank, and for a moment he thinks he might fall in. In his fear he gives a cry of alarm. Right behind him is Takis, hushing him and pushing him, but in his haste he too slips, and it is Spiros who reaches out a hand for him, pulling him on deck. But Takis remains staring at where he would have fallen, the black water reflecting the moon.

'I thought you said not to hang about,' Spiros slurs, eyeing up the cockpit seats as a possible bed.

'I dropped the spanner. Now shut up and get below. Let's see if there are any tools on board,' Takis hisses.

The hatch sticks and Takis has to manoeuvre past him to get it open. They practically tumble down the steps to the saloon together.

'Phew …' Takis exhales, and he sits on the nearest seat. 'Right, we need a torch … I saw one hanging here somewhere.'

He is on his feet again and feeling around in the dark. Spiros does not move. He has never liked the dark – the shadows move and you never know who is there. What if George has come back? There's a click, and a beam of light goes straight in his eyes.

'Sorry,' Takis mumbles. 'You look that side and I will look this.'

Spiros has already forgotten what it is they are looking for but he stands and rummages in the dark corners anyway, hoping that he might remember or spot whatever it is that Takis needs.

'Lift up the seats,' Takis insists.

He has taken up the cushions of the seat on his side. Underneath is a flat board with a hole in it, and by putting a finger in the hole he lifts the board. Underneath is a compartment full of tools: a tin of oil, a siphoning pipe, some engine spares. Takis searches by torchlight.

'Aha!' he exclaims and he pulls out a box of spanners. He selects two and takes them to the rear cabin and lifts up one of the floorboards.

'So I reckon if we unscrew that and release this hose we can just leave it and time will do the rest. Hold the torch.' He struggles with a spanner, cursing quietly. 'No, shine it where I'm looking!'

Spiros holds the torch and looks around him at the shadows. A strange dark feeling crosses his mind and he closes his eyes. Immediately he starts to drift, imagining his bed once again, and when he opens his eyes again he cannot quite remember why they are here or what they are doing, although something tells him he might end up in trouble and he does not like this thought.

'I want to go, I don't feel right.'

'I'm not surprised after all that ouzo you drank – now hold the torch still.'

'No, I mean, this doesn't feel right, what we are doing. I want to go.'

'It will feel fine when you never have to work again,' Takis says. 'There, that should do it. Now pass me that floorboard.' He replaces the board. 'Right, we're done, let's get out of here!'

Running back between the cars does not seem fun now, and as he climbs into Mitsos's truck Spiros makes up his mind that tomorrow he will at least apologise to Mitsos for using the vehicle without asking.

Takis starts the engine and they are almost out of Saros and driving through the orange groves before he puts the lights on.

'Ha ha!' He is full of energy and fun. 'We've done it! Now all we have to do is wait.' He slams both palms on the steering wheel.

'We must tell Mitsos we used his truck,' Spiros says. Tonight has not been fun – it has been strange and he is unhappy, but he is not sure what about.

'No! You can tell no one what we did tonight. No one, do you hear?' Takis's voice is sharp. 'Do you hear me, Spiro?'

The lights are switched off as they come into the square, and the truck is replaced exactly where they found it. Takis puts the keys back behind the sun visor and keeps his head down as they walk across the square and scuttle up the lane to their houses.

'Now go to sleep and don't mention a word to anyone. Sooner or later someone will tell us what has happened, and for George's sake looks surprised when they do!' And with this he steps into his own house, closing the door behind him.

Spiros looks up at the moon and has a desire to howl. It would relieve some of what he is feeling, but he doesn't. Instead he goes inside, flops on his bed, and for some reason that he doesn't really understand he cries until he falls asleep.

Chapter 6

The light through the window drives spears into the tissue at the back of his eyes. Spiros groans with the pain and turns over, burying his face in his pillow. Someone outside is drilling the road, pulling up the tarmac. He covers his ears with his hands but the noise is still there, and it takes a moment before he is aware the pounding is inside his head.

Turning over again he feels a tightening in his neck, and his feet seem to know before he does that he needs the bathroom. He kneels before the toilet just in time to grip its edges as yesterday's ouzo raises the water level. He heaves and retches until his stomach ties itself in knots, and even then it spasms again and he pants, trying to take control. Slowly the feeling subsides.

'Oh, Lord in heaven,' he groans, and he splashes his face with cold water from the sink. The reflection in the bathroom mirror shows no signs of anything he is experiencing. The pounding that was in his head is now more in his ears and the room is swaying.

'What did I do?' he asks his reflection, and he watches his mouth but no answer comes. 'What did Takis make me do?'

The events of the early hours begin to creep into his consciousness, each new image making him cringe. They stole Mitsos's truck and crept about in the shadows.

Oh! And they went onto George's boat, but why? That part will not come.

He brushes his teeth, takes a shower and brushes his teeth again. Then he puts on clean clothes, spends five minutes trying to get his hair to sit flat, makes a coffee, and only when he is taking his last sip does the memory of what Takis did last night come back to him.

'No!' He groans at the thought of George's beautiful boat at the bottom of the sea.

'Please no,' he repeats. Maybe there is time to save it, if he goes now, gets a lift into town, fixes the hose back on. But he doesn't know how. He rushes to the bathroom again and makes it to the sink just in time. By the time the spasms have quietened down, the back of his throat is sore and he desperately feels the need to lie down again. He cannot save the boat, not how he is feeling. Lying still is all he can manage. Sleep would be the best thing.

He is not sure if he wakes up because he hears a knock at the door, or whether the knocking starts after he has woken. He is sweating and is desperately in need of a drink of water. The knocking comes again, demanding his attention. He stands with care. His head is not too painful but he will not risk moving any faster than is strictly necessary.

Rap, rap, rap.

'Okay, I'm coming.' His throat hurts.

It's Babis the lawyer at the door. His face is serious; he does not smile but looks past Spiros into the house.

'Is Takis here with you?' he demands.

75

Spiros feels his eye beginning to twitch.

'No.' He leans on the door frame and looks out towards Takis's house. Babis, wasting no time, marches over and bangs loudly on Takis's door. It is opened more quickly than Spiros managed.

'Morning, Babi, how can I help you?' Takis stands tall, chest puffed out, hands in pockets, looking self-satisfied and showing no signs of last night's excess.

'Come over here, I want to talk to you both together.' Babis leads the way back to Spiros's.

Babis pulls out a chair and sits at the kitchen table without asking. He does not look happy. The place is still tidy as Kyria Isodia came only the day before yesterday. Spiros is glad of it as he has never had a lawyer in his house before and it feels rather intimidating. He does, however, wish he had had a chance to clean the bathroom and he desperately hopes Babis does not ask to use the toilet.

'Right, I am seriously hoping that what I am suspecting is not true,' Babis begins. The other two sit. Spiros feels nervous, but Takis seems calm, unconcerned.

'What are you suspecting?' Takis sounds mystified, but it is not genuine. He sounds like one of the actors in the black-and-white Finos films that he loves to watch. Spiros likes these too, although often the actors speak very quickly and Takis laughs at parts that don't seem all that funny.

'And already I'm beginning to think it's true.'

Babis looks at Spiros as he puts his hand up to his twitching eye. Spiros does his best to look innocent, but with Babis's gaze boring into him like that, it's hard to remember what his innocent face feels like.

'Please tell us what you are talking about?' Takis asks, sounding almost as if he really does not remember the terrible thing they did last night. 'Spiro, why don't you makes us some coffee?'

Spiros stands, grateful for the distraction.

'No, thank you, no coffee,' Babis snaps.

'I'll have one,' Takis says, and Spiros turns to the sink, takes two cups down from the shelf. He feels braver with his back to them and fills the *briki* as quietly as he can so he can listen to what is being said.

'It seems there has been an accident with the boat,' Babis says. He pronounces the word 'accident' very clearly and slowly. Spiros splashes water from the tap over his face.

Babis starts to speak again. 'The boat is sunk,' he says, and Spiros drops the *briki* in the sink with a clattering sound that echoes round the room.

'No! The boat?' Takis says, but there is no real emotion in his voice, no surprise. To Spiros it sounds like he has practised the words in a mirror. A dribble of sweat runs down his back.

'You guys are on very thin ice,' Babis says. There is a hard edge to his voice.

'Us? Why?' Takis sounds offended. Spiros refills the *briki* and sets it on the stove.

'I'm not going to ask, because if I ask and you tell me the truth then I am an accomplice. And if I ask and you lie to me I am none the wiser, so I will not ask at all. I will presume that the boat has sunk by an act of God, or a technical failing of some kind, and we will move on.'

Spiros spoons sugar into the *briki* and stirs it on the heat, watching the grains slowly dissolve. He then adds a heaped spoonful of coffee and the smell permeates the room. He waits for the mound of grounds to be absorbed. Making coffee is a soothing thing to do – you can't do anything else whilst you do it, apart from watching the bubbles form and taking care not to leave it on the heat too long. The trick is to heat the water slowly and whip the *briki* off the flame just before the coffee boils over.

As he watches the water, Spiros realises that the room has gone quiet, and he turns to find that Babis and Takis are staring at what he is doing. He feels his face flush hot, and a sizzling sound tells him the coffee has spilled over the edge and down the side of the tiny pan into the flame.

'Actually, I will have one,' Babis says.

'So, the boat has sunk, has it?' Takis asks. 'When we took it out there was a problem with the water inlet hose, and Aleko had to fix it, but maybe his fix was not so good.'

'You took the boat out?' Babis exclaims. 'But that isn't legal – the boat is not yours, probate has not been granted.'

'Oh, the port police said it was okay,' Takis says lightly.

'The port police said they did not want to know about it,' Spiros corrects, setting a coffee in front of Babis and returning to the stove.

'Please don't tell me any more, I really don't want to know.' Babis puts up a silencing hand. Spiros concentrates on making the second coffee.

'Okay.' The 'Lawyer for the People' takes a sip. 'So, let's hope for the best. Let me see the insurance papers. We'll file a claim – that would be the normal course of action following a genuine accident ...' Spiros turns at these words to see Babis looking expectant. Takis seems puzzled.

'But you have the papers,' Takis says. 'You are the lawyer and you have all the papers.'

'I have George's papers. I have George's insurance documents but ...'

'Well, there you go then!' Takis says confidently. Spiros sets a coffee cup on the table in front of him.

'Listen very carefully, Taki, as this is trying my patience. I have George's insurance certificate. It has George's name on it. Do you follow me? George is dead. The policy is void. It seems you might have done a lot of sinking without much thinking.'

The silence that follows is heavy. Spiros stands with the *briki* in one hand, motionless. Takis doesn't say a word, just stares at Babis, his lips slightly parted. Spiros looks from one to the other, trying to read the mood in the room.

'Yes,' Babis says finally. 'So if you didn't take out insurance of your own you have left yourself high and dry, or rather low and sunk.'

No one laughs.

There's another long silence, in which Babis finishes his coffee, and a thought occurs to Spiros.

'Couldn't we change the name on George's insurance to Takis?' he asks quietly.

Takis snorts.

'I'm afraid you cannot do that,' Babis says not unkindly. 'That too is against the law.'

Chapter 7

The sun is hot, the sky a sheet of deep blue, and there is not a breath of wind. The surface of the sea is smooth as oil, and so clear that Spiros can make out shells, rocks and even an old shoe on the bottom. These things are easier to look at than the bulk that is – was – George's boat. Not that the boat looks so different, really – rather that it doesn't seem right to see it from this angle, its outline wavy, undefined, with a veil of blue drawn over it.

The harbour isn't deep, and although the hull is completely submerged, the mast pokes out of the water, at an angle, and where it breaks the surface the water slowly rises and falls, and the smallest ripples spread in circles from it. This division above and below the surface sends flutters of horror into Spiros's chest. It makes him think of George, and how one minute he was alive and the next he was dead. He also thinks of himself. One minute he was himself, and the next he was a man who helped to commit a crime. There's no going back to being just himself now. The boat, just there below the surface, seems to shout this fact back up at him.

'Try to look sad,' Takis whispers. 'The port police are over there watching us.'

'I am sad. Why did you sink the boat? I liked the boat.' Spiros sniffs.

'You know why,' Takis hisses.

'But we can't have George's insurance money so I don't see why.'

'Just shut up and look sad for a minute more and then we will go.'

'I liked having George's boat.'

'It was going to cost us a fortune. We couldn't afford it, so just forget about it. Come on, we've been here long enough. Let's go.'

'Er, excuse me!' A man in port police uniform comes running up to them as they turn away.

'Quick, let's pretend we didn't hear him.'

'Kyrie Taki!' The port police man runs faster and it is clear that they will not be able to avoid him.

'Hello, officer.'

At this pleasantry the policeman clenches his jaw as if there is something he is trying to stop himself saying. He points towards George's boat.

'You need to get that out of there as quickly as possible. It's a hazard, dangerous to other boats, and we are having to keep watch to ensure everyone's safety because of it. So today would not be too soon to lift it out of there.' His jaw becomes tight again, and he turns on his heel and walks away.

'How will we get it out?' Spiros asks.

'I have no idea, the man's crazy. The boat's sunk, these things happen. How can we lift it out?'

Takis does not sound sure of himself, and he is no longer pressing for them to leave. Spiros is not sure now what they are going to do next. Takis has always given him the impression that he is smart, clever, but right now Spiros is beginning to think Takis's cleverness has got the better of them both.

As they stand there, a car pulls up and a tall man gets out; he comes over to stand by them, shaking his head.

'Bad luck, boys,' he says. 'I'm Maraveyas, by the way.' He hands Takis a card. 'I deliver water and diesel to the boats, although of course you won't be needing either of those just at the minute. But, you'll be pleased to hear, I also have a crane, and I'm sure we can get her out without too much fuss.'

'So if someone did want to lift her out, what would you charge for that?' Takis asks.

'Just to lift her? Well, there is the crane and the man hours, so it would depend on how quickly the job went.' Maraveyas seems satisfied with his answer.

'Roughly, ballpark figure,' Takis presses.

'Don't hold me to it, but I reckon we could get her out of there for – what, about four hundred euros?'

'Four hundred!' Takis sounds alarmed. 'For a couple of hours' work!'

Maraveyas shrugs.

'Of course, once we have her out we have to put her somewhere. I mean, even if we just put her right here, so there is no transportation cost, you will still need a cradle to support her. She won't stand on her keel and you don't want to lay her down.'

'A cradle?' Takis is sweating on his top lip. He wipes a hand quickly across his mouth.

'I could get you one made up, might take a while, a few days at the least, but I reckon we could do that for four hundred euros ...'

'Another four hundred!' Takis blanches and starts to cough.

'You okay, Taki?' Spiros pats him on the back. Takis waves a hand, coughs a few more times and straightens himself.

'Eight hundred euros!'

Maraveyas does not blink. 'I think I could manage with that,' he says calmly.

'We couldn't raise that money if we worked for a year and ate nothing but bread.' Takis looks down at the boat.

Maraveyas shrugs. 'Well,' he says, 'it would be less to lift her, but we'll have to get divers down there, now she's under the water, and bring her up slowly to let the water drain out ... And of course, the port police might not let you leave her here. Usually they don't, but they might make an exception for you. If not, we'll have to take the mast down and get her over to the yard on a truck, so that will cost more. You have to take the mast down because of the telephone wires over the road ...'

He starts to walk back to his truck.

'Let me know if you change your mind,' he says, and he climbs into his vehicle and drives away.

'It would have been cheaper to do all the repairs the boat needed than pay that money!' Takis splutters.

'What are we going to do?' Spiros's eye is twitching quite badly and the same muscle is now pulling at his cheek. He also feels a little sick. 'We should never have sunk her.'

'Don't ever speak those words out loud again, do you hear?' Takis turns on him with such anger, such venom, that Spiros steps back. 'You keep your mouth shut about that, we don't want criminal damage added to our trouble, you hear me?'

He points a finger at the end of Spiros's nose and glares at him in silence for a moment until a bead of sweat forms on Spiros's forehead. He dare not make a move to wipe it away; he is not sure what Takis might do next.

After what seems like an age, Takis drops his hand to his side and turns to walk away.

'Where are you going?' Spiros asks.

'To see Babis. I want to know if the port police can force us to take the boat out of the water.'

Spiros runs to catch him up.

'But they wouldn't tell us to do it if it wasn't the case.'

'If they consider the boat at the bottom of the harbour to be a problem they'll say whatever they like to make the problem go away, won't they?'

Spiros hurries after Takis and is panting heavily by the time they reach the lawyer's office.

'Right, we'll see what's what. You hold your tongue, say nothing at all, do you hear me?'

Takis is sometimes a little grumpy, but Spiros has never heard him speak this unkindly – not to him, not to anyone. He thinks he might stay outside and not come in to see Babis after all. But the image of the port police man comes to mind. He did not speak kindly, either. Maybe Babis can sort it all out? He is smart and is bound to find a solution. Spiros pushes past Takis and is first into the office.

'Spiro?' Babis says, sounding a little surprised. 'Where's … Ah, there you are, Taki. I didn't think you would be far behind. Come in, and shut the door.'

'The port police …' Takis starts before he is fully through the door.

'Shh, shh, shut the door!' Babis hisses, and he stands abruptly, hurrying around his desk and across the room to close the door himself.

'All right, all right, don't get so excited,' Takis protests.

'But what are you thinking? Do you want the whole of Saros to know your business?' Babis closes the door firmly and shuts the window too.

'Look, I didn't come here for a lecture from the likes of you …' Takis's voice is beginning to rise.

'And what is that supposed to mean, the likes of me?' Babis counters.

'Will you both just stop it!' The words tumble from Spiros's mouth, loud and heartfelt, and he is almost as surprised as the other two, who turn and stare at him open-mouthed.

'Be kind,' he insists, and for a minute there is a tense silence in the room.

Babis is the first to collect himself.

'Please have a seat, Spiro,' he says, flattening out his tie and resuming his seat behind the desk. 'Taki?' He offers him the other chair with a wave of his hand.

When they are all seated, Babis interlaces his fingers and rests them on the desk. 'Now,' he says, sounding serious, businesslike. 'What can I do for you?'

Takis leans forward and opens his mouth, but Babis holds up a finger.

'Maybe Spiros would like to tell me.'

'Me? Okay, I can, if that's all right.'

Spiros glances sideways at Takis, who is half turned away from him in his chair, arms crossed over his chest and a resigned scowl on his face, his lips a tight line. Spiros takes a calming breath and replies, 'The port police man says the boat is dangerous. Maraveyas says it will cost hundreds to do it. Can the port police make us?'

'Do what?' Babis says quietly.

'Makes us pay for a crane to take the boat out of the water.'

'Ah, I see. Well, yes they can' – as Babis says this, Takis takes a really big breath – 'and no they can't' – Spiros breathes out.

'So which is it?' Takis asks grumpily.

'As I say, yes and no.'

'I don't understand,' Spiros says.

'The boat hasn't gone through probate yet, so it isn't technically in your names yet. Officially, it is still in George's name so, technically, even though he is dead, George is responsible.

'Ah!' Takis sounds happier now.

'But as his inheritors you are the only people the port police can turn to, and as you will have, or rather would have had, a yacht in the harbour for the foreseeable future you would want to work with them rather than against them.'

'Aha!' Takis exclaims. 'But as we do not have a yacht we have no reason to keep good relations with the port police. Is that what you are saying?'

'Well,' Babis replies cautiously, 'that is one interpretation of what I am saying, and if it suits your purposes then it may be your chosen approach … But I believe you have the essence of the situation.'

'So we are off the hook!' Takis exclaims.

'I suspect the port police will not see it in quite the same way, but I suppose, if you really want to have nothing more to do with the boat, there is little they can do. After all, we are still within the four-month period,' Babis says.

'What four-month period?'

'From the day of death, the heirs have four months to revoke the inheritance and have nothing more to do with the whole process.'

'That! I want to do that!' Takis stabs his middle finger on the desk for emphasis.

'I thought you might. And you?' Babis turns wearily to Spiros.

'I have no money. What else can I do?' Spiros says.

'Okay, I will draw up the papers, and I'll see you in the next day or two.' Babis rubs his hands together as they stand to leave.

Spiros climbs the three steps into the *kafenio*. He's been out in the sun up on the hill minding Mitsos's goats and sheep all day, and now evening is drawing on. Despite the late hour it is still hot, and a nice cool lemonade from Theo's fridge would be welcome. Takis is already there, sitting by the window on his own. He has not seen Takis for the last week and doesn't really want to sit with him, but he feels obliged.

'Hello,' he says as he takes a seat.

'Haven't seen you around.' Takis doesn't look at him.

'I work for Mitsos now, herding his goats. I'm a shepherd.'

Spiros knows he should not brag, but he is still getting used to the idea that he has a title and an important job that carries with it a weight of responsibility.

'I'm glad for you,' Takis says, but he sounds miserable, not glad.

'Do you have work?'

'I dug a road for the council in Saros the day before yesterday.' He doesn't sound happy about this, either.

'That's good. Oh, here comes Babis.' Spiros watches Babis in his suit, sauntering across the square towards them. He looks hot.

Spiros expected Takis to be happy at the sight of Babis, who is after all helping them to get rid of the problem of the boat, but Takis sits and mutters under his breath and doesn't look at all happy. Perhaps after all he too is saddened by the thought of George's beautiful boat at the bottom of the harbour.

'Well, boys, I have the papers here to sign to revoke your claim.'

Babis pulls up a chair and sits, crosses his legs, uncrosses them, pulls down his sleeves, smooths his tie and runs a hand over his hair, pressing it flat.

'But I have been through some more of the papers that George left.' He leans forward and looks first Spiros and then Takis in the eye. 'And I suggest that you might not want to sign this boat away.'

'And why is that?' Takis says.

Babis looks about him cautiously and leans in over the table, speaking very quietly.

'It seems George was a smarter man than we thought,' he says, and the other two lean in towards him, to catch what he is saying.

'A man who was aware that life would not always be roses.' Babis seems to be enjoying himself, even though he is showing signs of nervousness, twitching and talking quickly. 'According to the papers, he was a smart man for a long time.'

'Can you just spit it out, Babi? What have you found out?' Takis says with impatience.

'Gold.'

'Gold?' Takis repeats.

'Yup, according to these papers he had almost a hundred gold sovereigns and a couple of gold bars.'

'You're kidding?' Takis breathes the words and Spiros smells the ouzo on his breath.

'Not kidding. Anyway, the point is that if you revoke the inheritance, you revoke the gold with it.'

Takis sits back at this, his eyes wide, and lets out a long, noisy breath. He runs his hands through his thin hair and shakes his head. Then, slowly, as if he is out of practice, a small smile appears on his lips, and Spiros is relieved to see his old friend looking happy. The smile is accompanied with a little chuckle, and the farmers across the room turn their heads.

'Okay,' Takis says finally, leaning forward and speaking very quietly, with a side glance to make sure no one is listening, 'so we don't revoke the inheritance, do we, Spiro?'

Spiros needs more time to let what has been said sink in, so he does not reply.

'Where do we sign?' Takis asks, slapping his hands together and rubbing palm against palm. He is grinning broadly now.

'You already signed the first time round. You don't need to do anything else.'

'So, how much are a hundred gold sovereigns and two gold bars worth?' Takis asks.

'Well, I estimate, after a little research, that it may be over thirty thousand. It depends on the purity of the gold bars.' Babis is whispering again. 'Of course, you cannot have the gold without the boat, but it is obviously more than you will pay to get her off the sea bed. Of course, once you have done that, you are also in a position to fix up the boat. Then you could sell her or work her, whichever you choose. And the nice part is that I don't think fixing her up will even make a dent in thirty thousand so you'll end up with the boat and the best part of the cash too!'

'Thirty thousand and the boat?' Takis breathes the words as if they are sacred.

'That is quite an inheritance,' Babis whispers back.

'Fantastic! So, when can we have the gold?'

'Well, any time you like, really …' Babis sounds just a little cagey.

'So where is it?'

'Well, you know George was a careful man …'

'A sensible man,' Takis agrees.

'Well, he was careful with the gold too, and he hid it.'

'Where?' Spiros asks.

'Yes, come on,' Takis echoes. He sounds excited, impatient. 'Stop playing games and tell us – where did he hide it? Let's go and get it, shall we!'

'Ah, well, that's the thing,' Babis says, his eyes flicking from Takis to Spiros and back again. 'He doesn't say exactly where he hid it, but I've studied the papers, and it's definitely in a safe place, somewhere on the boat …'

If you enjoyed *The Village Idiots* please share it with a friend, and check out the other books in the Greek Village Collection!

I'm always delighted to receive email from readers, and I welcome new friends on Facebook.

https://www.facebook.com/authorsaraalexi

saraalexi@me.com

Happy reading,

Sara Alexi

Printed in Great Britain
by Amazon